BOOM

TOWN

A NOVEL

by

Anthony Cannon

GRAND UNION PUBLISHING

First Edition - 2016

Copyright © 2016 by Anthony Cannon

Cover Design by Anthony Cannon

ISBN
0995634009
978-0-9956340-0-8

The author would like to acknowledge that the chapter set in the casualty clearing station is partly based on the war memoirs of Doctor John A. Hayward.

GRAND UNION PUBLISHING
23 Kelross Road
London N5 2QS
grandunionpublishing@yahoo.com

ABOUT THE AUTHOR

Anthony Cannon was born in Arklow, County Wicklow in 1967 and has lived in London since 1990. He has a degree in History and English. *Boom Town* is his first published novel. He spent several years researching the Kynoch factory and has written about it in the magazine *History Ireland*. He is currently completing his second book, a crime novel set in Dublin in the 1970's.

TO MY FATHER AND CHRISTINE

CHAPTER 1

Dusk was turning to night when she left the small terraced house. Around her head was a dark woollen scarf that she wore partly against the cold and also to disguise her from any neighbours. In her left hand was a thick cloth travel bag belonging to her mother. Inside was everything she possessed - two dresses, two shawls, a pair of boots, some coloured glass jewellery and some items of underclothing. She squeezed the frayed leather handle as she walked along beneath the glowing gas lamps. There were no lamps at the end of the street. Beyond it was too dark to be recognised unless someone offered a greeting and she replied.

The day shift at the factory wasn't over for another hour and she met no one on the road out of the town. She didn't look back as she took the bend and her house went out of view. There were few things behind her she wished to remember, and yet, it was not easy to go. Still she refused to entertain thoughts of why she should stay. She had made up her mind, there would be no turning back. She came to the brow of the railway bridge and she imagined she heard the train and it set her heart to racing. It was only her nerves putting her on edge. The train wouldn't leave until seven, filled with men and women from the factory. And once she and Thomas were on it they were free.

She continued over the bridge. A man on a pony trotted by. He raised his cap and watched her as she hurried on. She was a mysterious figure no doubt, a young woman with a bag on a journey all alone in the pitch-black. The man might be tempted to come back and enquire. She rushed on, all the time watching for

1

the narrow path and the place where she and Thomas were to meet. It wasn't far ahead. In the daytime the spot was as familiar to her as any other part of the town. In the night however, it was difficult to see and she was afraid she might pass it without knowing.

Then the man commanded his pony to halt. He was returning the way he had come. He would catch up with her in no time. She hoisted up her skirt and began to run. The man in turn gee'd up the pony. So she ran yet faster and stumbled. She was sure she was done for but she had fallen by the opening to the path. She picked herself up, flung the bag over the wooden gate, scrambled up and over after it and hid behind a bush until the pony had gone down and back up the road.

About a hundred feet up the path was a clearing with a fallen tree that was used as a seat. She set herself down there and waited for him to come. To some it would have been an opportunity for reflection. Mary, however, thought not of the past, or of the future. Her mind was fixed on the present and getting away. She had decided that they would not return to the road until ten minutes before seven. It would take precisely eight minutes to get to the station and they would remain on the bridge until the train could be seen on the long straight stretch coming up from Wexford. Only then would they go into the station where they could hide in the crowd thronging the platform.

After a short while she heard him approach from the opposite direction she had come. She got to her feet and prepared to embrace him. There was an unexpected break in the clouds and she could see him clearly in the bright moonlight. He brushed aside a branch that lay in his path. He was about to speak and she raised her hands to his mouth.

Be quiet, she whispered, and she offered him her lips.

They kissed briefly and he muttered some words in a distracted and off-hand manner.

What's wrong? she asked, even though she was well aware of the answer.

She knew him well enough by now, and it was plain enough on his face that he didn't want to go, that he was almost fearful. His bag weighed him down as if it was filled with rocks and his eyes were searching for a place where hers would not find them. She saw a boy, not a man, someone who needed to be led and shown the way. She thought she could show him, in return for his loyalty and devotion. The chore was not easy, now especially, her nerves were ragged and she was close to losing her temper at his mumbling, incoherent response to her question. He was afraid to speak out, to admit his uncertainty about the wisdom of their actions. It had taken quite a bit of persuasion on her part to convince him that it was best for them both. At times he agreed, and there were other times, such as now, when he very much doubted it, and if an excuse not to go were to come his way he would have happily been bound by it.

Do ye want ta go or don't ye?

He was slow to reply. As much as he wanted to stay he did not want to disappoint her. This, however, could not alter the fact that he was afraid of what lay ahead. He was afraid of going to England. And why did she want him to go? Because she loved him, as he did her, or because she couldn't go alone or she needed his money? And how was she so sure that they would have a better life there? She told him there would be work in the factories because all the men were off to the front. And what if the war ended soon as many had predicted?

Well, she said, yer not comin den, is dat it….fine!

Ah Mary, he said in a weak, almost pleading voice.

No, dat's fine Thomas, I'll go by meself, you might be frightened, I'm not.

How can ye go by yerself? he said, sure yer only a young girl on yer own.

3

She was ready to unleash a few oaths. She held them back. She had gotten him this far, surely she could get him another step further, then another and another. But she was too tired to repeat the old arguments all over again, so she stroked his arm and took him by the hand.

Come on, she said, and she tugged him.

He took several steps forward and baulked.

There were angry voices nearby. A man was coming down the path from the road.

Mary went to take the other path. Someone else was advancing this way, ripping and tearing at the branches as they went. She took her bag and plunged into the thorny bushes that surrounded the clearing in the hope that she could circle around and come out onto the road. Thomas followed. It was loyalty that made him stay by her side. It was certainly not a desire to escape, and when the hands of Mary's brother and father were upon him, pulling him back into the clearing, he made no attempt to struggle or resist. When she saw that he had surrendered she gave up and she was hauled back through the ditch by her father with such force he ripped the seam of her jacket sleeve.

Let go a me, she protested.

Hush now, said her father, and he held fast to her wrist and with the other hand he deflected the fist she threw at him.

Yer hurtin her, said Thomas.

Mind yer own business, said Mary's brother, and he stood between them to prevent Thomas interfering in any way.

Ye tink I'm hurtin her do ye? said her father, not-a-tall, she's well used to makin a hullabaloo, she's always at it.

I said let go a me ye drunken pig, said Mary.

What a way for me precious daughter ta be talkin ta me, said her father.

Do sometin Thomas, said Mary.

Dat young chap isn't goin ta do a damn ting, are ye Thomas? said her father.

Won't ye let go of her, said Thomas, over the head of Mary's brother.

Wahu, said her father.

Mary's wild fist had come within an inch of her father's right eye.

Ye gotta watch dat right hook of hers, he said.

Help me Thomas, said Mary, and he lunged at Mary's father.

He was thrown back by her brother, and when Thomas had withdrawn, her brother stuck his thumbs in his pockets, cocked his hat back and spat on the ground.

Jaysus Michael, don't just stand dere like a feckin' gobshite, said her father, grab a hould a yer sister and take her straight home.

Huh, said her brother, she's as crazy as a bull dat one.

Is she now? he said, and he clouted her hard across the side of her head.

She'll behave herself now, continued her father, she'll get a few more licks just like dat if she doesn't.

Yer mad men, said Thomas, the both of you.

Dere's no other way ta control a girl like dat, said her father, and he repeated his order for Michael to take hold of her and take her home.

Me scarf, she said, and she tried to pick up the scarf that had fallen from her head during the struggle.

Never mind dat, barked her father, pointing towards their house, take her home, me and young Thomas are goin ta de pub ta have a friendly chat.

Don't listen ta him Thomas, shouted Mary, as she was dragged off, he can't stop us doin what we want to do.

Her words were of no use. Her father's friendly invitation had just the disarming effect he'd intended. The boy was easily

5

charmed into silence, and her father, still hot and panting from the encounter with his daughter, threw his arm over the boy's shoulder and led him away.

Her mother was asleep in the sprung chair by the fire when she was disturbed by the ruckus outside. She bent over to pick up the rosary beads that had fallen from her grasp as she slept. She dropped them into the pocket in her apron and was heading for the door when it flew open and her daughter was thrown into the house by her brother, who bolted the door as soon as he was inside.

The woman staggered backwards in shock at the violence of the entrance and she held her heaving chest as her two children faced each other like mortal enemies.

Michael looked at his mother and saw her pitiful and bewildered expression.

She tried ta run off, he said, hoping this might in some way justify the viciousness of his actions.

She was gonna take off with dat Thomas fella, weren't ye, he said, and shoved her against the wall to frighten her into a confession.

The mother turned to her daughter.

Tell her, said Michael, go on, tell her.

Her mother's eyes fell to the stone floor, she shuffled around the chair and went silently towards the tiny room at the back of the house where Michael's bed was.

What? said Mary, in response to her brother's hateful stare.

What? she said a second time, with even more contempt and her brother raised his arm to strike her. She flinched not a fraction at his threats, rather she offered her cheek and told him to do as he wished, and his fist, driven by all his fury, descended onto the table and the pieces of Delph all neatly arranged for the evening meal jumped several inches into the air. Most of them

6

landed back on the table, those that didn't went to the floor and were smashed.

Oh Lord bless us and save us, said their mother, and she put her hand up to the wall to steady herself. The terrible din, the condition of her daughter and the animal rage of her son was more than she could bear and she collapsed in the doorway between the two rooms.

It took a moment for her children to come out of their mutual anger and they raised her up, one arm each, and took her up the narrow staircase to her room.

They put her on the side of her bed and she sat there gasping for a breath of air.

Mary drew the curtains and told Michael to go and get the doctor.

I will not, said Michael, I'm stayin right where I am.

Go Michael, said their mother, and she began coughing again, Mary won't leave me, will ye Mary?

No, said Mary.

Da told me to take her home and keep her here, said Michael.

Do as yer told, said their mother in a spontaneous eruption, and her son left the room reluctantly with a promise to be back in five minutes.

Mary pulled back the sheets to coerce her mother into bed.

Ye never should've got out of it in de first place, she said.

Sure I had ta cook your fader's and Michael's dinner, she explained.

Why can't yer husband cook his own diner, said Mary, he's notin else ta do.

Her mother was about to answer and Mary told her it was not important.

She helped her mother undress, fetched some turf, put it on the fire and told her mother to try and sleep.

I can't, said her mother, and she moved about in the bed restlessly trying to find a position that was comfortable. After a lot of tossing back and forth she did sleep, only for a few short minutes and she was wide awake.

She squeezed her daughter's warm hand.

What are ye tinkin about? she asked her daughter.

Mary didn't want to answer.

Tell me, her mother insisted.

I was rememberin, said Mary.

What were ye rememberin?

When ye were fit and strong, said Mary.

I was well able for dose two men, she said, and I got no lip from Michael before I was ill either.

The clock on the mantelpiece chimed the half hour.

Ye like dat auld ting don't ye? said her mother, and she asked Mary to wind it a little.

Mary took the key from the cup of knick-knacks and inserted it carefully into the mechanism.

Don't overdo it, her mother warned.

Mary sighed and smiled.

Yev told me the same ting a million bloody times, she said.

Well I'm tellin you…

Her mother halted mid-sentence and clutched her throat. Her head shot back, she drew some air in through her nostrils and a spray of blood exploded from her mouth and onto the bed cover.

Mary took the damp cloth that was kept in a bowl by the bed for such emergencies and she wiped her mother's mouth. With the other side of the cloth she wiped the bed cover as best she could. She showed no outward signs of anguish or distress. She had seen it many times before. Her only thought was that it could be all over and her mother would cease to suffer.

Where's yer father? asked her mother, clutching her rosary beads.

The latch on the front door was lifted and Mary said that might be him.

Steps pounded up the stairs and Michael appeared at the entrance to the bedroom.

Well, said Mary.

Well what? said Michael, irritated at the abruptness of her enquiry.

Is de doctor comin or not? she asked.

He's with auld Fogarty, he said, cocking his hat, he'll be here in about an hour.

He leaned against the doorpost, crossed his legs and lit the end of a half-smoked fag.

Don't smoke in here, said Mary, wafting away the cloud Michael had blown carelessly into the tiny room.

Why not?

Ye know damn well why not, she said, it's bad for Ma's chest.

If you were so bothered about her health, he said, why did ye run off like dat?

Her mother's eyes opened like a pair of heavy old doors.

I told her ta go, she said.

Mary noticed how dark her eyes had become.

I told her ta go, repeated her mother, in case the young man had failed to listen to her the first time.

Do ye hear me? she continued, and eventually Michael nodded and her eyelids fell closed.

Michael went and got more turf for the fire and piled it in a big heap in the grate.

How did ye find me? asked Mary, rubbing her mother's hand.

Dat fella on de pony, said Michael, did ye not recognise him?

No, said Mary.

Jaysus, he said, in a long hiss, well ye shoulda done, it was yer uncle Seamus.

Mary shook her head and cursed her bad luck.

He sort a recognised ye, but it was dat auld bag dat really gave ye away, he said gleefully, it belonged ta his mother ye know. Even in de dark he spotted it. Dere's not another one like it in de whole world accordin ta Seamus.

Her mother had grown still, and except for the laboured rise and fall of her chest she was entirely without motion.

Ye best go and get Da, whispered Mary.

Michael narrowed his eyes and gave her a quizzical look.

Well, I'll go den, she said, getting to her feet.

Ye'll do no such ting, he said, ye stay right where ye are now, don't budge an inch unless de doctor comes, I'll be right back.

He thundered back down the stairs, slammed the front door behind him and the two women were left alone once more.

After a while her mother sat up. She was wide awake and lucid.

Can I have a glass a water honey? she asked, and Mary poured out a cupful from the jug on her mother's dresser. She took the cup and drank it down until it was empty and lay back on the nest of pillows her daughter had made while she was sitting upright.

Were ye really going ta leave me, her mother asked.

Well I don't blame ye, she said before her daughter could reply, dat awful factory….

She wanted to speak further, but she hadn't the strength, she needed to rest.

The room was getting feverishly hot. Mary opened the window. Outside the whistle of the train was shrieking. It always seemed to express some sort of joy to Mary, even as her mother lay dying beside her. The joy of motion, of leaving things behind, of the possibilities and opportunities of other places. That simple sound conjured all these feelings. She imagined the trudging of the train, the rhythmic clickety-clack of the wheel on the track.

Just thinking of it she experienced a thrill in her breast as she imagined plunging fearlessly through the night.

I always loved dat sound, said her mother, and she put her hand on her daughter's arm.

Ah look, she said, yev ripped yer lovely jacket, I'll mend it for ye in de mornin.

Yes, said Mary, you can mend it in de mornin.

.

CHAPTER 2

Michael sat alone in the gloomy, yellow-lit canteen of the factory. Occasionally a man would slap him kindly on the back or offer a firm hand of condolence. It had been two months since his mother's funeral and still they approached him every day. Men utterly unknown to him, men without names, and invariably they would say how great a woman she had been and how much she would be missed. For all these well-intended remarks there were other not-so-generous words that circulated behind his back. Some were envious of his mother's industriousness, of her prosperity, and they were glad at his family's misfortune and pitiful decline since her illness and death. But even the kind words only really served to heighten his own sense of worthlessness and helplessness. If he had listened to his mother and taken to the books she was so keen on he would have done far better for himself. In the end her nagging had made no difference. He had no appetite for learning, anymore than he had a head for business or being a shopkeeper as she had been.

He stared out the window. In the distance, on an expanse of low grassy sand dunes, was an assortment of buildings compressed together into a little town. They were all constructed from the same dreary grey concrete. Michael remembered the day the great industrial enterprise called Kynoch came to town like a terrible carnival. The local priests and the politicians were falling over themselves to thank the owner from Birmingham. Michael saw the owner, Mister Chamberlain, in the courthouse on the day of the big meeting to decide if the town wanted the factory or not, and all the people cheered *we want work, we want work*. Michael thought Chamberlain every bit the English gentleman - tall, thin, cold, and contemptuous. Still, he was amazed at the enormous machinery being hauled through the town from the station, all heading for the beach and in less than three months the untouched emptiness where he had played as a child was transformed.

Dey've got everytin in dat factory, his father had said, a laboratory, a library, sure dey've even got a fecken billiards room so ye can pass de hours readin and smokin fine sea-gars from Cuba and playin games like proper gintlemin. Ye have ta hand it to em, dem auld Brits are quare smart, it's no wonder we've been under de cosh for so long. His mother disagreed. It's not because dere so clever, she said, it's because we're so stupid. Funny kinda nationalist you are? said his father, and he was very pleased at the apparent contradiction he'd illuminated in her philosophy. De truth, if ye want ta hear it, replied his mother, is dat dey've built an almighty mess, and Michael agreed.

Two men sat down in front of Michael with trays of hot food.

Michael acknowledged the men with the slightest of nods.

What's up with ye? said the small, skinny one whose name was Seanee.

Notin, said Michael, and he took a sup from his mug of tea.

Everytin more like, said the fat man, whose name was Jimmy, and he chuckled at the irony of his observation.

He's been up half de night by de looks of him, said Seanee.

Michael pushed down his unruly black hair. The man was right. He was tired. He rarely slept more than three or four hours and then he was forced to get up. His bed offered little rest, only bad dreams and by the time he was awake his was as exhausted as when he had laid down. Over and over Jimmy had told him that the cordite they handled was harmless and Michael would get used to it. It wasn't true. The moisture from the paste was

13

burning the skin on his hands. His belly never stopped aching. He was irritable and his eyes itched and stang constantly. His sister had bought oil from the chemist and he'd rubbed it into his hands every night. It had done some good for a time and then it had ceased to have any effect. The only relief was seawater. His father swore by it. It was a cure for every ailment under the sun, he said. Michael would steep his hands in a basin of tap water mixed with the salty liquid and rinse his eyes with it most evenings. But there was no real remedy to be had. The factory was poisoning him, of that he was sure.

Dis is grand grub isn't it? said Seanee.

He was talking with his mouth full and Michael could see the chewed-up food moving around inside.

Ye eat like a fecken horse, he said.

If it wasn't for dis canteen he wouldn't eat at all, said Jimmy, and he slurped up a spoonful of his vegetable soup.

Well ye eat enough of de slop yerself, said Michael.

I do, do I? replied Jimmy.

Yer not denyin it are ye? said Michael.

Jaysus, I've had enough outta you, said Jimmy, ye do a whole lot a talkin and not a lot a listenin.

Michael shifted in his chair and presented Jimmy with his shoulder.

Yer not still goin on about what happened de other day are ye?
said Michael.

If dat nozzle jams dat cylinder could blow up, said Jimmy, and it'll take all tree of us to hell with it.

It won't blow up, said Michael, it won't explode unless it's in a bullet, dat's why we make de damn stuff.

And what do ye tink dat cylinder is only a giant bullet? said Jimmy.

14

Do what Jimmy tells ye, said Seanee, and he tapped Michael's upper arm playfully.

A group of men sat down at the far end of the table. All of the men were from Wexford and worked in the nitro houses. They were rarely seen. The buildings were at the far end of the beach and the explosive was usually made at night when there were fewer people around and the air temperature was lower.

Heard yez had a little panic in de press house, said the man nearest Jimmy.

Ahh, it was notin really, said Jimmy.

The man leaned back in his chair.

I heard you was pissin yerselves in dere, he said.

Well ye heard wrong, said Jimmy.

I used to work on dem presses in England, said another man from Wexford, dere quare dangerous if ye don't know what your doin.

We know what were doin, said Jimmy

I seen one of dem presses go on fire, continued the Wexford man, and he removed a pair of thick goggles that had been sitting on his bald head and he wiped the smudged glass with a filthy rag.

I'd say it was probably de same type of press too, he went on, about tree foot tall. We used ta pack the cordite paste in dere and dat screw came down nice and slow forcin de paste through the nozzle and out she came in lovely, perfect long narrow strips. Worked a treat most of the time, as long as de paste was de right consistency...when it wasn't...

Ye hear de man, said Jimmy through his teeth.

Well one day, the Wexford man went on again, dis batch came in, a whole truck load of it, dry as desert sand it was. Cordite paste's lovely when she's wet, when she's dry it's not good boy. Anyway, we rammed dis paste in de cylinder in small handfuls, forced it right down so it was good and compact,

15

started up de screw, and down she came pressin the paste, and out she came like milk out of a juicy udder, until it had gone about halfway, and it stopped. We could hear these little screams comin from de cylinder. It was the sticky paste forcing itself against de polished side. Den dere was a sharp crack, like sometin hard had snapped, followed by a heavy thud dat shook de whole machine. I swear, I taut de press was goin ta break free from its mountings, and I'm countin under mc breath, ten, nine, eight seven…still notin was coming out…six, five, four three, two...but dat nozzle, she'd completely blocked. And then I got ta zero. Shut her off, I shouted. Give it another second, said the eejit operatin de screw. SHUT IT OFF, SHUT IT OFF, IT'S BLOCKED. Me face turned a dark shade of red and me hair was standin on end like a crazy animal. FUCKIN TURN IT OFF YE STUPID CUNT. De men at the other press were cowerin and were gettin ready to leg it. De foreman was runnin up from de engine room ta see what all de commotion was about. I went ta yank dis gobshite away from de lever and shut it off meself. Too fuckin late. Dat nozzle shot off de machine and hit the concrete floor. Dere was a flash and sparks and de whole ting caught fire and de chap operatin de lever was...well, dat stuff burns hot, really hot, especially if it's anyway dry, it practically melted him.

All the men round the table were silent.

Jaysus, said Jimmy to Michael, now do ye believe me?

I heard ye de first time, replied Michael, and he stood up abruptly and kicked his chair back out of his way.

Jimmy's eyes shifted up from the table and he fixed them on Michael. They were a cold blue colour, all washed out, and watery and ghostly.

He lay his spoon down calmly.

If ye don't like it, he said, you can work with someone else.

Go fuck yourself Jimmy, was Michael's response.

I'll teach you, he said, and he was up before the words were out, his hands curled up tight like rocks.

Seanee grabbed a hold of his belt and pulled him back with all his strength.

Lads, lads, he said, come on.

Michael was already well out of range of Jimmy's large fists.

Ah sit down ye big eejit, said Michael.

Don't push it me boy, said Jimmy.

Michael showed him his back and went to get another cup of tea.

Seanee and Jimmy watched Michael as he sauntered off and joined the queue for food.

Go easy Jimmy will ye, said Seanee, de boy's lost his mother.

I don't remember him singin her praises when she was alive, said Jimmy.

And did ye ever hear im say a bad word agin her either? asked Seanee.

Well, said Jimmy, I suppose not.

Dere ye go den, said Seanee.

Ah, he's stubborn and stupid, said Jimmy, one minute he's sour de next he's as giddy as anytin.

Were you any better at his age? said Seanee, a great deal worse I'd say. Wild as a boar you were. Now he's got de message so lave em be.

Right, said Jimmy.

And we'll be outta dat place soon enough, said Seanee, dere's work going in the dryin houses.

No tanks, said Jimmy, with a disapproving snort.

Suit yerself, said Seanee, and he directed Jimmy towards the queue.

Standing waiting for food was a group of noisy young women.

Ah the freshness of youth, said Jimmy, with a broad sorrowful smile.

Too young for us, said Seanee.

Not for yer man though, said Jimmy.

Michael was moping around behind the women. They were talking rapidly amongst themselves, swapping sarcasms and bitter remarks. Michael was hoping to talk with them but they didn't seem to notice him at all. They were doing it deliberately, he thought, ignoring him. Dat was the way of women, especially the tall one called Rose whose attention he sought the most.

He fell back a step and one of the girls cast a sly glance at him.

She started to giggle.

Ah, would ye look who it is, she said, and all except the tall girl said hello.

The line of girls was broken, a space was made for Michael and he was in the midst of them. Some of them said they were sorry to hear that his mother had died and others asked where Mary was.

Well, said Michael, she didn't much like it in the factory so she's got another job housekeepin for Doctor O'Connell.

What? said Rose, dis job isn't good enough for her? I'd never be a skivvy for someone.

Ah, be nice, said one of the older girls.

She's only messin with ye, said another, she wants the attention, don't ye Rose.

I can get all de attention I want, said Rose.

The queue was moving and the girls formed into a single line. Rose was directly in front of Michael and in an impulse he took her arm and she allowed him to pull her back, but she refused to face him.

What are you doin for your lunch break tomorrow? he asked, do ye want to go for a walk on de second beach with me?

18

I might do, she said.

I'll meet ye outside here at noon, said Michael, and I'll take ye for a walk. Will you be here?

Maybe I will, she said, and maybe I won't.

Seanee and Jimmy were watching Michael with admiration.

She's a fine figure of a girl isn't she lads?

They looked down the table.

Sitting furthest away was a young, good-looking chap called Der Earls. His head was resting on the table in a childish yet menacing way.

Can't say much for her choice of company though, he added.

Jimmy was heating up. His big square jaw came out about an inch.

Lave it Jim, said Seanee.

The words fell out of the side of Seanee's mouth slyly, like nothing had been said at all.

I'll get a few of em before dey take me down, said Jimmy.

And what about me, said Seanee, dey'll tear me apart like a scarecrow.

Jimmy sucked in some air through his nostrils.

Well, he said to Der, sometimes ye just end up with company ye don't like very much.

The man nearest to Jimmy was filling his chest in preparation for an abrasive response when a loud whistle cut through the noise of the busy canteen.

A foreman was standing by the door and he signalled to the Wexford men that it was time to go and he walked straight back out again.

I tink you boys better be runnin along now, said Jimmy.

Ye, said Seanee, with an exaggerated nasal whine, yer mammy's callin ye.

We'll see you round, said Earls, dragging himself up off the table and the others followed.

19

Not if I see ye first, said Jimmy, and he waved them off with a regal twist of his wrist.

CHAPTER 3

Mary shivered in her thin nightshirt. The house was cold and dark and silent. The months of coughing and wheezing from down the landing had ceased. It was replaced for a short time by her own sobbing in the wee hours. After a few days that too had ceased. Her mother was gone and so was Thomas. She had cried her heart out for them both and when all her crying was done she stopped and there was no more mention of his name and rarely any mention of hers. As for Michael, he never cried, not even when his mother lay in a coffin in the front room.

She dressed and went downstairs. Her father was sleeping in the sprung chair by the fire with an old blanket thrown over his knees. He'd snored his drunken head off until around two when the nasal symphony had subsided to a soft whistle. Sitting snugly in his lap was a half-empty bottle of Guinness and his stocking feet rested on the hearth stone with the toes on display. On the table were several empty bottles and fag butts were thrown indifferently to the floor. The fire was still warm and when Mary stoked it she unearthed a few embers. She threw a lump of turf on, found some bread and butter in the press, boiled up some water to make some tea and sat by her father chewing on the stale crust.

She stirred up the fire. Seeing the poker in her hand brought back memories of destroying her mother's bedclothes in the back yard.

Burn it all, said the doctor, burn everything, even her clothes.

After that Mary had made the place spotless for the wake and the neighbours who came and went could see all the fine pieces of furniture their mother had bought. And as they stood by the side of the heavy oak coffin with the shiny brass handles they all looked down on her one last time and they said that when it came to business there was no better woman. It was true. Mary and Michael's lives were good, thanks to her. They had more than most. Then the sickness came and everything went bad.

After a long while she stood up on a stool and searched on top of the press to retrieve the few coins she'd hidden there. Her hand moved gently over the thick dust and her fingers crept towards the wall. She found the stack of five pennies. She dropped them into her purse, put her coat on and was halfway out the door when her father, still half-asleep, uttered her name repeatedly. There was an urgency in his tone and in his shaky hand was a letter.

It came yesterday, he explained.

Mary snatched it from his fingertips and left.

No sooner had she set foot outside than her neighbour stepped out of her front door and was calling after Mary in some jumble of mumbled words and Mary was saying sorry, that she was late and couldn't delay.

Ah, stop for a minute will ye, she demanded, and she ran after Mary and took her by the wrist.

She was a queer sight, and a pathetic one, with her shabby black shawl thrown carelessly around her head and shoulders and a pair of workman's boots with no laces or socks on her feet.

I'm late for work, said Mary.

Ah just listen ta me for a minute now.

The woman always had a great story as to why she hadn't two bob. Mary indulged her anyway. She even gave the appearance of being interested. Inside, however, she was screaming to be free, and once she sensed that the end was coming she produced her purse.

The woman cupped her hands together tightly and hunched her back.

I'll give it back ta ye when Jimmy gets paid, she said.

Mary took out the two pennies and placed them in Mrs Dempsey's waiting palm.

That's it?

That's yer lot, said Mary.

The very minute he gets paid, said Mrs Dempsey.

Right so, said Mary, and she thought, as she always did, that the more reassurances that were offered the less likely it was she would see those pennies ever again.

Here, take this, said Mrs Dempsey.

It was an amulet made out of bits of wood and leather.

I don't believe in dat auld stuff either, said Mary.

Ye don't have to believe in it, said Mrs Dempsey, you just have to keep it with ye.

No, said Mary.

Suit yourself, said Mrs Dempsey, and she stuffed it back in her pocket.

And how's Mrs O'Connell? she went on, hoping for a morsel of gossip about Mary's employer that she could dish out over a drink in her kitchen with the neighbours later on.

Have ye ever heard any idle talk outta me? said Mary.

The woman didn't answer.

Precisely, and I'm not goin ta start now, said Mary.

She's a bit odd, you'll grant me dat, said Mrs Dempsey, with a cheeky grin designed to tease something out of the girl.

Yer a bit odd, said Mary.

Ha, scoffed Mrs Dempsey, holding the coins up, dey can talk about me all dey like, as long as I got a bit a dat I couldn't give a hoot, and off she went.

23

At the end of the street Mary tore open the envelope. She had no need to guess who the letter was from, it could only be Thomas.

Almost immediately it started to spit rain and she replaced the letter in the envelope. She consoled herself with the prospect of stealing a few minutes out of her morning routine to read it. As she walked she thought how much she missed him. She passed by the grassy path where they had met the night of their attempted elopement and the loneliness and the sadness of his absence crept upon her like a terrible chill. She shrugged it off. It was pointless to torment herself. What good would it do to hurt herself this way? So these feelings were smothered and extinguished.

She walked down the Main Street, over the bridge and up the hill. She stopped at the first house she came to. She pushed the gate open, mounted the steps and knocked. Standing at the window, his head barely visible, was Doctor O'Connell's son. A few seconds later he was shoo'd out the door by the wizened and bad-tempered housekeeper, and his hand slid into hers and he walked along contentedly by her side.

Between the road and the factory down below was a small wood of very tall evergreen trees. The boy craned his head upwards at the slender giants.

Dat's where all de crows live? he said.

Yes, said Mary, dat's where de scary crows live.

Who lives in dat house? asked the boy.

He was pointing at a long shingle building on the far side of the wood overlooking the factory.

Dat's de hospital, said Mary.

Mary could see a group of patients in striped pyjamas by the entrance, puffing away on cigarettes. The place seemed to be trapped in the long, dark shadows of the trees.

Is it for de people who are ill? asked the boy.

24

Yes, said Mary, de factory makes dem ill.

De factory where dey make de bombs?

Yes, said Mary, where dey make de nasty bombs.

A little further on were more grand residences, many of them occupied by the families of Englishmen who worked as managers in the factory.

Look, look, said the boy, and he squeezed Mary's fingers.

Up ahead were a handful of soldiers, some of them on horseback. They were drawing two heavy guns up to the garrison at the coastguard's house.

A soldier stood in the road barring the way.

He removed the cigarette that was dangling precariously from the corner of his mouth.

Mornin, he said, with a smile that made him appear very handsome, and he explained that they would have to wait until the guns had been moved in off the road.

Mary went and sat on a wall with the boy.

My name's Jack, said the soldier, and he raised his cap by the peek and bowed in an exaggerated fashion that was silly and flattering.

Mary could feel his soft hazel eyes shining at her, drawing her towards him, and his smile had grown, infecting his whole face, causing Mary to experience a rare and very annoying sensation of shyness. She was not keen on flirting, and certainly not with an English soldier guarding an English owned factory that was making explosives for an English war.

She was about to take out the letter once more when, as if by magic, the soldier produced a small paper bag from his tunic pocket.

Would you like one? asked the soldier.

He was offering the boy a sweet.

Can I take one? he asked.

I suppose so, said Mary, and the boy reached inside the bag and removed a bit of sticky toffee.

And wot about the pretty young la-dy? asked the soldier, and he rustled the paper and winked at her.

No, de young lady doesn't want any, she said, and she crossed her arms and legs into two tight knots.

Can I have hers? enquired the boy timidly.

You'll ave to ask the young...

Oh for goodness sake, go on, interrupted Mary.

I want ta join de army when I grow up, said the boy, my daddy's a soldier.

No he is not, said Mary, he's a doctor.

I'd like ta go to de war, said the boy.

You need to stay at 'ome and take care of your mother, said the soldier, and he helped himself to one of his own sweets.

My mother's dead, said the boy.

Sorry to 'ear that young man, said the soldier.

I'd like ta shoot a gun, said the boy.

Oh, ye don't wanna do that, replied the soldier with an intense frown, someone might shoot back and then you'd be dead.

Why are you one den? asked the boy.

I've been conscripted, said the soldier.

Conscripted? repeated the boy.

It's a bit like the way you've been told to go to school, he said, well I've been told to be a soldier by the King.

Mary was trying not to listen. She rubbed her ankles. Her feet ached from the long hours standing washing and ironing. And there were holes in her shoes. She had mended them herself with a bit of old leather and done a poor job of it and when it rained her feet became wet and cold. She had the money to buy a new pair, but instead she kept it, squirreled it away, soon she would have enough to go away alone, and she'd never come back.

The second gun was disappearing between the gates of the coastguard's house and the way ahead was almost clear of men and horses. Mary tested her feet against the ground. The brief rest had helped to ease the pain.

Come on, said Mary, before the soldier could finish answering the question the boy had asked.

She got down off the wall and walked briskly. The boy struggled to keep up and he started crying.

Whist with yer whingin, said Mary.

What are ye running for? he asked.

I'm not, said Mary, yer legs are too short.

And then, without warning, she came to an abrupt halt. Someone was at the doctor's gate. At first she took the woman for a visitor. It never crossed her mind that the person might be the doctor's wife, Catherine, until she recognised her hair tied up like a captive beast in an awkward bundle at the back of her head.

She watched Catherine progress along the footpath away from her. She moved quickly and Mary detected in her hurried steps some panic. Four soldiers met her on the footpath. They stood aside, gave her a respectful salute, and when she had passed they admired her slim figure. Catherine gave no visible reply, she kept on going towards the factory entrance on the north beach.

Where's she goin? enquired the boy, who was just as intrigued as Mary.

I've haven't a clue, replied Mary, and she released the boy from her grip and he ran off to the next house to play with the neighbour's little boy.

Mary took her key, opened the front door and hurried inside. The house was warm from the previous day's fires, and it was quiet, but it was not peaceful. Even before the doctor had gone off to the war Mary suspected it was an unhappy place. She remembered the first day she came. The doctor warned her, Catherine is a very particular type of woman. She is an artist, he said. She doesn't trust people easily, he said. The doctor hadn't lied. From the very beginning Mary found her moody and unpredictable. So much so that she could never tell from one day to the next what kind of reception she would receive when she stepped through the door - a door where the world she knew and understood ended and another, altogether stranger one, began.

Once inside Mary instinctively began searching for a sign that might explain why Catherine had left the house, and in such haste. She went through the downstairs rooms sweeping back the heavy red velvet curtains and the daylight poured in but she found no clue to her departure. She thought that she might find something in the bedroom. She went to the bottom of the stairs, and hesitated. It was not a place she ever went unless summoned.

Mary was shocked the first time she laid eyes on the bedchamber. It was dirty and untidy. Dust lay thick on the marble mantelpiece, and everywhere else she looked. Half-read books and discarded magazines were thrown about. The dresser was strewn with jewellery and perfumes. Stuffed inside the enormous wardrobe were dozens of expensive dresses, so many that they were spilling onto the floor. The clothes were remnants of Catherine's life in Dublin, a life occupied with dressing up and socialising. Now Catherine hardly went out at all. She had no friends and, apart from her mother-in-law whom Catherine disliked intensely, she had no relatives in the town. She existed almost entirely within the confines of the house. After her morning coffee she got up to paint. The walls of the bedroom were decorated with Catherine's own works of art. Mary thought them strange and grotesque. Her afternoons were whiled away lying on the chaise longue by the front window, the bedroom door slightly ajar, and she would read or could be heard talking and laughing on the phone to some mysterious friend. Then, around five Mary would be beckoned to light the fire and tidy the bed, and for the remainder of the day the burning coal was Catherine's only companion.

But recently even these solitary activities had ceased. She slept through the mornings and all her afternoons were passed in her darkened room in her bed. She read no books, she received no calls. Mary preferred not to contemplate what dark thoughts occupied the woman's mind on the long, lonely evenings once Mary had departed. On the bedside table, in a dark green bottle, were Catherine's sleeping tablets. Every Monday she would ask Mary to go into town to order the coal, to collect the paints delivered from a shop in Dublin, and countless other small things, and finally, pretending it was an afterthought, she would hand Mary a small pink slip of paper, her prescription. It's less sleep yer needin not more, that's what Mary wanted to say to her. And the girl in the pharmacy, thinking they were for Mary, told her to go easy on them, dey'll knock ye out and ye'll never wake up, she warned.

Mary repeated what the girl had said and Catherine laughed.

Are ye worried I'll die and you'll have ta go back and work in dat horrible factory? she said.

If dat's what ye want, said Mary, ta go ta sleep and never wake up, go ahead, and if I have ta go back ta de factory...well, I'll go back, and dat's dat.

Mary had lied. She remembered with painful vividness the factory and the work she did there - four hours at a time on her knees on a cold concrete floor in front of the machine that filled paper cartridges with gelatine. The machine made a nightmarish hypnotic clunking noise. Even when she had left the factory she still heard that rhythmic clunking. The explosive powder was stronger than any domestic starch or bleach. It dried into the skin making it flaky and itchy. The machine itself was far more dangerous. She had to work frantically to keep up with it. Every few seconds the heavy steel mechanism would rotate and a fresh

29

load of cartridges was spewed out. An error of judgement or a moment's distraction and the monster would eat up a hand or an arm mercilessly. That was the fate of another young girl who lived on her street. She was left mutilated and unable to do work of any kind. And in the midst of all this hardship Mary found no consolation or comfort from her fellow workers, not the female ones. She was isolated and alone. They conspired against her, bullied her and left her to sit by herself in the canteen, and so she sat through her daily ordeal, a conspicuous solitary figure.

Her foot was still on the first step of the stairs. She drew it back. Catherine would be back soon, Mary was certain of it. So she gave up on her spying, and set about her household chores. She dragged the large rug from the hallway through the dining room and kitchen, out into the garden and threw it on the hedge. Catherine didn't seem to notice how filthy it had become. Mary wondered if she noticed anything at all. Except for her meals, the fires and the weekly shopping list, she gave Mary no instructions and she was allowed to conduct the business of housekeeping as she saw fit. It suited Mary fine, she was in no need of supervision, and everything was done as well as it could be.

The only thing she ever complimented Mary on was the funny little childlike drawings of the neighbour's dog and the boy that Mary sometimes did while she was drinking her tea.

Oh Mary, dere excellent, said Catherine, and Mary bit down on her tongue and held back a sarcastic comment.

Mary continued beating the rug until it refused to offer up any more dirt and she hauled the heavy carpet back through the kitchen and laid it down on the pretty ceramic tiles.

She was tired from the exertion. She decided to make herself a cup of tea. Then she sat down at the kitchen table and filled with a nervous, unsettling excitement, she laid Thomas' letter out before her. After all the earlier anticipation she couldn't bring herself to read it. She was angry at being forced to wait so long for a communication, and she was afraid of what it might say, and then she hoped it might say the very words she dreaded and she would be free and not have to wait anymore. She cursed all men. There wasn't a decent one of her class to be found in the whole of the town. They were all like her brother, hard men, or so they all thought anyway, who liked to drink and fight, and were good for nothing. The only exception was Thomas, and if she was honest, he was no great shakes either. He was so shy she had had to court him herself. He simply didn't understand what a woman wanted, practically or with regard to the physical side of things between a man and a woman. He would always have to be told. Her father had despatched him with no difficulties, and off to sea he went with the promise of Mary's hand in a year. Her father knew full well that the boy who went away was never coming back, if he came back at all. And the only decent looking fella who'd expressed an interest in her was the soldier. He was no good either. She would have nothing to do with him. He was a British soldier. The mere thought of him and she was overcome by the fire of anger and nationalistic pride in her belly.

She took the unread letter, crumpled it up slowly and went to the fireplace in the dining room. On the mantelpiece was a box of matches. She removed one, struck it firmly against the box and let the flame caress the edge of the letter. The paper was consumed in seconds.

CHAPTER 4

The fragments of ash were falling gracefully onto the tiles in front of the grate when the front door opened. The doctor's wife had returned and Mary was suddenly alert. She wasn't alone. She was accompanied by a man. It was the first time Mary had heard a male, other than the doctor, speaking inside the house. There were whispers in the hallway and the guest was ushered out into the garden. Then Catherine glided into the dining room, her cheeks red and radiant with the kind of happiness that only children really experience.

Oh Mary, yer here, she said, and she kicked off her shoes and she came and stood over her.

Her tiny pink feet were bare. Mary looked up and was struck, as she had been before, by her beauty. She could see how such a woman, difficult as she was, might be very alluring to men. She was young, far younger than the doctor and perhaps only two or three years older than Mary herself, and she possessed a childlike quality that made the doctor, and Mary, somewhat protective towards her.

Don't ye tink ye should put on some slippers?

The woman's head dropped heavily and she lifted it again.

I like being in my bare feet, she said.

Mary nodded dubiously as she shovelled the ash into a tin bucket. She was waiting for an explanation about the guest. None was offered. Catherine simply flew out the door like a bird and was gone as quickly as she had come.

She returned to her guest in the garden. Even from a distance her almost hysterical voice could be easily distinguished. Mary could sense her excitement. She was speaking too quickly. She didn't finish her sentences. She was giggling. She was like an over-wound mechanical toy. Mary expected the spring to break at any minute and for her to topple over. And there was something familiar in it all. The words she used, the lilt in her tone, a playfulness Mary had never been a party to.

She went into the pantry to deposit the ash and then she peeked through the tiny window onto the garden. She spied Catherine and the stranger sitting side-by-side on a seat at the end of the lawn in the warm sunshine. He was a handsome, well-dressed man of about thirty with thick, black hair and small eyes. The man's right arm was resting casually on the back of the seat behind Catherine. The neighbour's dog was sitting at his feet. He was rubbing the animal's floppy ears. Mary had no idea of the man's identity and she felt his presence and his casual familiarity with his surroundings were a kind of intrusion.

In the man's hand was a cigarette and when he turned to exhale the smoke he saw Mary. He smiled uncomfortably at her. Catherine was too preoccupied with her own talking to notice the brief exchange and her maid stepping away from the tiny window.

Mary experienced nothing more than a slight tinge of embarrassment. She told herself that it was expected of servants to be nosey. Their trivial lives were so dull, or so their masters believed, and they were probably flattered when their servants eavesdropped and gossiped about them, like the stars of the stage production looked upon from afar.

Catherine flew back into the house and went to the pantry door. She was rubbing her arms. They had changed to an ugly shade of pink from being exposed to the fresh air.

A friend of my husband's has come to see me, she explained quickly, and Mary could see she was annoyed at having to account for the visitor.

She rubbed her hands together vigorously to warm them a little and she asked Mary to prepare some tea for the guest.

Yes, of course, said Mary.

You can serve it in the drawing room, she said, and she disappeared up the stairs.

Mary brewed the tea, took down the best china and put it on a silver tray with some biscuits.

When she entered the drawing room she found the man bent over and peering into the doctor's large telescope with both hands behind his back as if he was afraid to touch the instrument.

He spun around swiftly.

Mary, isn't it? he said, and his arm shot out to shake her hand.

Mary stared down at the tray and the man laughed, apologised, and pointed to the low table in front of the couch.

Mary looked into the mirror above the mantelpiece as she set the tray down and saw the man looking at her the way that men often did, perhaps without even knowing it.

Oscar, he said, and he presented his hand again.

His palm was warm and dry and soft, and he had a vague scent of cologne.

Seeing him up close he seemed short and a bit untidy, in a deliberate way. He wore no tie, his linen shirt was open at the neck, and his suit was slightly wrinkled, not as the fashion dictated. He was how Mary imagined a writer or an artist to be. His smile and manner appeared free and easy and from first impressions he seemed disinterested in class and so-called proper behaviour. His looks, she thought, were boyish, almost feminine and he was probably shallow and vain. He was the kind of man a woman could have a good time with, not marry. His accent was a curious and uncertain mixture, Anglo-Irish was how Mary

34

believed it was referred to, a fancy expression for something that was neither here nor there.

All this Mary worked out in an instant and from her piercing and intense expression the man, if he had any intelligence at all, would have realised this. Not that he cared. As Mary had guessed, not caring was part of his personality.

After his greeting there was a clumsy silence, when the man, to his own surprise, wanting to say something and keep Mary in the room, found himself lost for words.

Mary was edging towards the door, her curiosity satisfied. Her fears of an intrusion were, she now realised, unnecessary. The man, whoever he was, far from being threatening was harmless and didn't really wish to be in the house at all.

He glided over to the mantelpiece and rested his elbow there.

Won't you pour de tea, he said, I'm awfully awkward with dese things.

Mary went to the low table.

How would ye like it sir? she asked.

Wet, said Oscar, and he chuckled at his own stupid joke.

Mary didn't respond, if this was Anglo-Irish humour, she thought it very poor indeed.

Sorry, said Oscar, scratching his head in the place where he always scratched when he'd done something foolish.

Any way at all is fine for me, he continued, and Mary poured the tea and milk and stood rigid, awaiting further instructions.

You have got a terrific view of de factory here, he said.

I suppose, said Mary, it's a terrible place really.

Where's a terrible place?

Catherine was at the door tying the ribbon to a tiny straw hat she was now wearing.

If ye don't like it, well you can always…

No, no, interrupted Oscar, and he took a couple of nimble steps around the table to stand at her side, we were talkin about de factory ye silly woman.

What about it? she asked.

Dere's no need to be huffy now, said Oscar, and he raised his arm to give her a reassuring embrace.

She allowed his arm to rest on her shoulder while she finished making a little bow beneath her chin and on her face was a smile of victory. And just in case Mary had forgotten, there followed a subtle reminder, wrapped in benevolence, of Mary's situation.

Yer week's money is on de table in de kitchen, she said.

Right so, said Mary, without any affected air of gratitude.

Shall we go? said the doctor's wife.

Yes, said Oscar, and he drank the hot tea in one mouthful.

CHAPTER 5

They left the house and crossed the road. Oscar walked north towards the factory and the beach. Catherine didn't follow. She remained opposite her house and was looking down the hill.

I want ta go inta town, she said.

Her mood had changed from euphoria to argumentativeness. She wanted to confront him. She was jealous of the maid or angry at the conversation they had on the phone earlier that day. The mere suggestion that he might be 'going away' had brought her running to his door. Or it might not have been this at all. Any trivial thing would do as long as she could torment him in some way. He had not known her long, long enough though to be familiar with her capriciousness. In the garden they had agreed to go along the beach. But her change of mind was not to be questioned, not if he wished to avoid a falling out and perhaps even then, when he had agreed to go into town, where he didn't wish them to be seen together, she would find some other reason to fight with him.

And I suppose if dat's what ye want den dat's what we must do, he said, and he waited for her answer.

If ye don't want ta come with me I'll go alone, she said.

He found himself growing angry at the thought of being bullied and if it had not been for the motorcar that was coming up the road he probably would have descended into a bad temper.

The motorcar came to a squeaky halt beside Oscar. The man behind the wheel was his cousin, Peter. He was wearing an army uniform. He gave the doctor's wife a very stiff salute, at which she beamed with pleasure. She was obviously beside herself over the shiny contraption.

Dinner's at five sharp, said his cousin, and you've got orders to be dere.

Oscar sighed as if some heavy responsibility had been laid upon him.

Just be dere, said Peter, and he prepared to move off.

And where are you off ta? enquired Oscar.

Business near Rathdrum, said his cousin, and he released the long brake lever.

Won't ye take us along for de ride? asked Catherine.

His cousin was not quick to respond. He was too polite to object and in his hesitation Oscar saw deliverance from his immediate predicament.

Well now, dat's an excellent idea, he said, offering Catherine the front seat, and he climbed into the back and leaned forward between driver and passenger.

Ye know de doctor's wife don't ye?

Yes, yes, said Peter, and he yanked at the brake lever and negotiated the machine into a jolting forward motion.

He was using this operation to distract himself from his annoyance and in the process was doing both very badly.

Oscar fell back in his seat. He was enjoying his cousin's discomfort. Both men were keenly aware of what the other was thinking, in particular the fact that Oscar had, as usual, gotten the better of his cousin.

Catherine was oblivious to their petty rivalry. She was gasping with fear and a kind of exhilaration as they headed towards the hill. Peter was attempting to gain control of the vehicle. A family with small children were walking on the side of the road. The mother grabbed her beloveds and held them fast. Peter steadied the steering, the gear however was too high and they raced down the incline much faster than he had intended, leaving the onlookers with the impression that the driver was a dangerous fool, and the screaming passengers were no better.

Peter applied the foot brake gently at the bottom of the hill, pulled over and applied the handbrake firmly.

Bloody hell, he said, I could've killed somebody.

Dat wouldn't do at all in your line a work, said Oscar.

I'm a little out a practice, said Peter.

At killin people? said Catherine.

At drivin, said Peter.

Come on now, said Oscar, as if he was herding cattle, get dis beast movin.

Yes, said Catherine, and she rubbed her knees impatiently.

Peter set the machine rolling again and it ambled gracefully over the bridge.

The old fishermen gathered on the southern bank of the river waved as they passed by and swung right on the busy Main Street.

They were immediately confronted by a herd of sheep and the machine was reduced to a crawl.

Dat factory is a miraculous boost ta local business, said Peter.

It's a boom town, said Oscar, every eejit has money to spend, especially on de auld drink, God bless em.

Dese people always have money for dat, said Catherine.

Dere not your people den? asked Oscar.

Definitely not yours, said Peter to Oscar.

On dat point, said Oscar, I can neither confirm nor contradict you.

Children were gathering around the motorcar and Oscar saw an unusually warm look on Catherine's face, or maybe it was not unusual at all, it was simply that Oscar had not expected it.

Just after the post office the sheep were pushed and shoved down a lane and Peter shifted up a gear. They chugged up the hill passed the courthouse, and the church and the children ran after until they grew tired and gave up.

They took a sharp right at the top of the town. The road followed the course of the Avoca River along the bottom of a winding valley. Thick, luscious trees decorated the sides. Beside the river the valley floor was an almost perfectly even surface of fertile fields with crops and cattle. Catherine was thrilled to bursting point. The open air and the sensation of power and speed went completely to her head. Even the endless bouncing in and out of enormous holes did not seem to bother this normally squeamish and delicate woman.

Faster, faster, she said, we need to go faaaaaster!

Not a chance, said Peter, it's too risky, and it's not my car, it's his fader's.

I couldn't give a damn about the auld man's car, said Oscar.

Still, he went on, de good bits of road are very slippery from last night's rain, we could end up in de ditch.

Dat's unusually sensible for you, said Peter.

Well, it's like dis, said Oscar, de last time he loaned me dis ting I smashed de front headlight and I killed de neighbour's dog, and I haven't heard de end of it since.

They passed the village of Avoca and a mile further on the valley tightened into a slender gorge. They were approaching the copper mines and the scene changed completely. The valley's sides had been stripped of trees to reveal orange-brown rock and clay beneath. It was as though the skin had been torn away, revealing the raw and tender flesh. Great chunks of hillside had been gouged out and huge piles of dusty earth were deposited on the man-made shelves that formed giant steps up the valley's flanks. Smoking chimney stacks for smelting dotted the landscape and filled the air with a smell of burning wood. Peter clunked and ground into a lower gear. Lines of men, many of

40

them Welsh, walked along the roadside. They were tired and filthy.

More raw materials for the war, thought Oscar. Copper for the shells and bullets. Men toiling underground to supply the men above with the means to kill each other. How absurd the whole thing was.

Not for you me boy? shouted Peter.

A hard day's work in a subterranean hell, no, not for me, not if I can help it, replied Oscar, in a rather vacant way and he lit a cigarette and blew the smoke into the wind as they rolled on through the valley.

A few miles up ahead was the Meeting of the Waters, a place where two shallow rivers flow languidly into one another. Overlooking this beauty spot was a pub and a small crowd was sitting on benches outside enjoying the view.

Can we stop here for a little while? asked Catherine.

Peter's left arm shot forward to reveal his watch.

I'm sorry, he said, I'm really pushed for time here.

Why don't ye just drop us off, said Oscar, we'll have a stroll around and you can pick us up on de way back.

The motorcar was stopped unceremoniously, the passengers off loaded and Peter was on his way to Rathdrum to conduct his urgent business.

Would you like to get some tea? asked Oscar, or something stronger maybe?

No, said Catherine, and she offered him her hand.

She was taking him over a stile and down to the river's edge.

Oscar held back. He didn't wish to be intimate and yet he couldn't resist her gentle coaxing and he found himself being led down to a secluded spot under an oak tree. She sat on a patch where the grass was dry and patted the ground for him to sit by her. He seemed reluctant and she pulled him by the trouser leg and he sat obediently. The excitement from the drive had yet to

41

subside. She couldn't remain still and as Oscar lay back she began to talk while he listened.

Her mood was transformed once more. She was yet another woman. She wanted to talk freely and openly. It was as if she had to explain about her life, to explain things that were very important, and there wasn't enough time to get it all out, like a door to the outside had been thrown open briefly and she had to step through it as quickly as possible before it was closed and she was a prisoner once more.

She talked about her brother who had died in an accident when he was only sixteen, and her father and their long, happy summer holidays together in Donegal. She even talked about her husband, the doctor, and she recalled with a crooked smile how he had pursued her. But mostly she talked about her miserable childhood, a succession of frightening nannies, and her mother, a beautiful and glamorous woman. And as she spoke Oscar knew that sooner or later the door would close, the darkness would come and she would return to her cold and distant self.

I never heard ye speak about yer husband before, said Oscar.

I try not ta, she said, he isn't here, de war isn't here, dey may as well not exist.

Ye may not see it, said Oscar, but de war is very real.

Are ye frightened of de Bolsheviks? she asked.

In a way, he said, and de war will wipe us out.

Us?

De upper-classes dear, he said, affecting a tone of femininity, and de socialists will do de rest.

We don't belong ta any class.

We'll never free ourselves from what we were born inta, he said, especially in dis bloody Catholic country, people won't let us.

We could go to London?

Neither of us have any money, said Oscar, and what about yer husband?

He might not....

She didn't finish her sentence and he said no more, and in the long painful silence that followed, the little that remained of her earlier excitement fizzled out and died. Oscar did nothing to try and revive it and she became listless and finally morose. No kind or amusing words were offered to cajole her or lighten her mood.

She got up and went and sat on a stone. She wanted him to join her, to comfort her somehow, but he couldn't comfort her. His words would be false and she always seemed to sense it whenever he lied. How idyllic it all could have been, two lovers together in this enchanting place. It would be perfect, if she was not married and he was not poor. He wondered if he did love her, and whether he would marry her if he'd had the chance? He doubted it. He was too immature, too selfish and too lazy. And she would have him at his wits end with her moods, or worse still, the bouts of madness he'd heard about.

She got up from the stone and he followed her further along the river's edge, still not saying very much until the roar of the motorcar engine was heard. Peter was on the bridge waving and beckoning them.

They drove back along the same route. No words were said between them. The afternoon had become overcast, the scenery now appeared drab, and all three were immersed in their own troubling thoughts. Peter dropped his two passengers where he had picked them up and a few polite words passed between them. More than anything Catherine wished for an expression of devotion, something ardent and passionate. He wouldn't give it. He looked about uneasily as if being in a public place was preventing him from some display of affection. He touched her hand discreetly, kissed her on the cheek the way mothers kiss their children. She asked if he would come inside again and he

43

muttered something about having to attend dinner and they parted.

Oscar walked through the gates, passed the motorcar and up the gravel drive to the front door of his family home. He remained there for a moment while he considered his appearance. He decided he would go upstairs and put on a tie. He opened the outer and then the inner door and stood quietly in the hall. To his right was the dining room. His father was talking in his usual tedious way to the unfortunate dinner guest. Oscar moved past the open door towards the stairs. He'd risen halfway and his mother was calling him from the dining room. She came to the bottom of the stairs, leaned against the newel post and wrapped her hands around the ball that sat on top.

Mister Cocking is here Oscar, she said.

Yes, I heard him, said Oscar.

I thought you were trying to escape, she said.

To where? replied Oscar, dere's no escape in dis house.

Don't delay, said his mother, you're already late.

He mounted the remaining steps and went down the landing.

His cousin was sitting on the bed in the spare room directly opposite his own. He was removing his boots and uniform. He had altered greatly since he'd gone away to the war. The gentleness and calmness that Oscar was so jealous of were still there, but struggling to maintain themselves. On the table by the window was a bottle of whiskey and a well-charged tumbler was by its side, quite an adjustment for someone who previously had rarely drunk. Black rings had formed underneath his eyes. Oscar only acknowledged the freshness of his cousin's youth now that it was gone. At times he drifted off into his own world and was hardly aware of where he was at all, and Oscar heard him wake from his sleep screaming and shouting incoherently.

You were born for army life really, said Oscar.

What makes ye say dat? asked his cousin with slight amusement, I never would've taut so.

Ye haven't missed a single meal since you've been here, said Oscar.

I like yer housekeeper's cookin I suppose.

Oscar picked up the tunic his cousin had removed.

What's it like?

What's what like?

De front?

You've never enquired before, said his cousin.

I never wanted ta know before.

Oh, it's too gloomy, some other time, let's go and have some dinner.

Oscar was by the window drinking the whiskey from his cousin's glass.

Three horses were trotting past the house. They were returning from a hunt and the riders were caked in dried mud.

Dat's your future down dere, said his cousin, if ye stay in dis town. Horse riding, shootin at weekends, courteous invitations ta cold and drafty country houses, dressed up in formal attire for de evening. Perhaps ye'll meet a pretty young woman from a good family.

And de shame of explainin my position workin as a clerk for Mister Chamberlain? asked Oscar.

Oh ye'll be alright, said his cousin, yer accent and manners are passport enough.

If I have any position at all, said Oscar, with any luck Mister Cocking won't like the cut of my jib.

Perhaps, said his cousin, and now we have ta go downstairs and talk politely to the bastard.

Indeed, said Oscar, the bastard dat helps supply the killin machines dat make all the carnage and destruction possible.

CHAPTER 6

Michael was sitting on a narrow plateau on top of the Spion Kop, the headland that marked the end of the north beach and the factory. He lay down in the tall grass and sat up again in a state of mild panic. He ransacked his pockets until he found the tiny box he was looking for, and he settled back down. He closed his eyes and tried to capture the tranquillity he had experienced a moment before while looking up at the perfect blue sky. It was gone. His mind had drifted back to his earthly concerns. He was impatient to see Rose. He flipped over onto his belly, parted the grass and looked down at the track that wound around the back of the nitro houses. Perhaps she wouldn't come. Then a weight was suddenly on his lower back and his head was pulled back roughly by the hair.

He flipped over violently and saw Rose fall on her side and roll towards the edge. Michael reached out to grab her. But she threw her arm in the air out of his reach.

He crawled over beside her and peered over the precipice. It was a sheer drop of fifty or sixty feet onto the jagged rocks and sea below.

Jaysus, he said, ye nearly went over de side.

Rose lay on her back laughing.

So what if I did? she said, dat would be a great way ta die, smashed ta pieces and carried off by de waves.

If ye wanted ta die I suppose, said Michael mildly.

He rubbed the back of his head.

46

Dat was bloody sore, he said.

Yer lucky I didn't bite ye, she replied, gnashing her strong white teeth.

Yer like a wild animal, he said.

Maybe I am, she said, and she twisted her long fingers into a claw.

Ye tink dat's funny do ye?

Some lads like it dat way, she said, and she ran her nails down his cheek.

What do ye mean, what lads? demanded Michael, de ones from Wexford?

No one in particular, she replied absently.

No one in particular, repeated Michael, it's dat fella Earls dat was admirin ye in de canteen, ye fancy him don't ye.

What would ye do if I did? she asked.

Michael refused to answer. The words were stuck in his mouth and he wouldn't let them out.

I taut ye were my girl, he said eventually.

And what gave ye dat silly notion? she said, because I've come up here a few times?

What's silly about it, said Michael indignantly.

Is it yer pride or yer heart I've hurt? she enquired solemnly.

Yev got a strange way of talkin.

And yev got a strange way of carryin on.

I taut ye liked me, he said.

Not when yer bein like dis, she said.

Like what?

Boring.

I suppose dat fella from Wexford isn't boring? said Michael.

If yer just goin ta nag me I'm goin ta go, she said, I get enough a dat at home. It's either dat or de auld fella's beltin me around de place for no reason.

Well I want ta know where I stand, he said.

47

What does it matter? she said, I'm here with ye now aren't I?

And who are ye with when yer not with me?

No one, said Rose, and she rubbed his chin affectionately.

Give me a kiss? he said, lowering his mouth towards hers.

Get off me, she said, and she pushed him away and giggled.

Give me a kiss?

Shh now, she said, settle down, I was up half de night with me little broder screamin.

But…

She put both of her hands firmly over his mouth.

Let me rest for a while, she said, and she nestled her head in his lap and closed her big green eyes.

He was glad to let her sleep. He could admire her features. And looking at her resting made it possible for him to believe she was something other than what she really was, lazy and selfish and stubborn. She'd admitted as much herself.

Michael's hopeless preoccupation with the more fiery variety of women had not gone unnoticed. They'll be the ruin of ye, his mother had told him, if ye don't become master of yer desires and not always be a slave ta dem.

We're rarin a right eejit, she complained bitterly to Michaels's father.

Don't be at de lad constantly, was his father's usual reply.

Shut yer gob, was his mother's riposte. When it comes ta women it's not tenderness or affection or kind feelings dat de boy is after, not-at-all, it's a hot-tempered shrew with a pretty face, a narrow waist and all de other bits I'm too ashamed ta mention. At this point his father invariably hid away in a quiet corner and let her 'blow herself out' as he put it.

Yer lucky ta have some guidance on dese matters, she said, when I was your age no one told me anytin about life. I had ta work it all out for meself. And tanks be ta God, I was born with

48

half a brain, dat's one half more dan yer fader over dere, and I used it ta get on.

Michael listened to the waves below. He let them drown out his mother's scolding and then all he could hear was the roar of the white water crashing against the rocks. He looked up the coast. To the north was another beach that flattened out into a wide stretch of sand and then high dunes. Behind the dunes the land quickly rose up into a semicircular slope. It was like an ancient open-air amphitheatre covered in a tangle of small trees and thorny bushes. Continuing north there was beach after sandy beach as far as the eye could see, all the way to Brittas Bay. It was a beautiful sight in the afternoon sun and it filled Michael's chest with a light and dreamy sensation.

He heard a slow, heavy blast coming from the quarry on the other side of the river and he turned back to the south and the munitions works. From the top of the headland the factory looked like a battlefield covered in craters with shacks plonked inside. In between these endless mounds were thick concrete tunnels built above ground. There were bogey tracks everywhere, thirty-seven miles of them in total. Pipes ran from one end of the beach to the other supplying acid from the old chemical factory by the mouth of the river to the nitro houses. Everywhere Michael looked there were barrels and tanks of lethal acids and some days their awful smell was carried on the sea breeze and would hit you like a phantom.

His father tried to defend the factory. He said that the people wanted jobs.

Hah, said his mother, cordite, dey talk about it like dat devilish stuff is manna from heaven.

What difference does it make? argued his father, de people want work.

No good would come of it, that was her ominous prediction and there was proof enough for anyone who needed it. The

49

hospital was full of sick and injured men, caused by burns from the acids. It was no surprise to Michael. The workers were being made to work faster and faster, night and day, to produce more explosives for the front. And for such dangerous work the men received a mere fifteen odd shillings a week.

Michael turned to the smaller beach again and surveyed the grassy dunes. Here and there were faint plumes of cigarette smoke rising up in the still air. It was the Wexford men from the nitro houses. A few minutes passed and they were getting to their feet in ones and twos and walking up and down the sand hills towards the headland.

Michael shook Rose. She grunted her disapproval and refused to move. He shook her harder and she lifted her head like it was a great weight. It flopped forward and she opened one eye then the other.

I was havin dis lovely dream, she said.

What did ye dream? asked Michael.

I can't really remember, she said, it was lovely whatever it was.

The Wexford men were climbing the rocky path up the side of the headland and into the cut between the headland and the mainland. Rose watched them about twenty feet below as they walked abreast in twos and threes. At the end of the cut they met the dirt track down to the nitro houses.

We better go soon, said Michael.

Rose stretched her limbs to their full length and was about to get to her feet.

Wait, said Michael.

Of course, said Rose, we've still got time, and she pulled him down onto her by the collar to kiss him.

No not dat, he said, drawing away.

He fished the small wooden box out of his pocket and offered it to her. She raised herself up on her elbows and looked at him

50

with disappointed eyes. What's dat? she asked suspiciously, it's not what I tink it is.

It might be, said Michael.

She took it and she stared at it. It was painted a glossy black and had gold trim around the edges.

Aren't ye going ta open it? said Michael impatiently.

There was a little spasm in her throat and she lifted the lid.

Michael studied her expression. It was not the delight he had hoped for. She was amused, nothing more, and it was belittling for him. But when she examined the ring she let out a tiny gasp and her dimples appeared.

Where did ye get de money for dat? she said.

Never mind, said Michael, I bought it for you.

Well, I don't really care where ye got de money from, I'm not takin it, she said, and she replaced the lid and returned it to him.

Why won't ye take it? he said.

Because dat's not what I want from you, she said, and she took his hand and placed it on her breast.

Michael pulled it away angrily.

Don't ye like them, she said, and she moved her leg in between his and was rubbing the inside of his thigh.

I want ye ta marry me, said Michael.

Wouldn't ye prefer something else, she said, and the tips of her fingers were travelling slowly up inside his shirt.

Don't do dat, he said.

Is dat not what ye want? she asked, we can do it up here, no one's goin ta see us in de long grass.

Will ye marry me? he whispered.

Don't ye want sex? she said.

I want ye to be mine, said Michael.

Dis is what all de other boys want, she said, and her other hand was moving towards his crotch.

You're a bloody auld whore, he said, and he clouted her hard across the side of her head.

She didn't recoil. She struck back instantly with her fist and it cracked against his nose and his left eye. The little black box with the gold trim fell and the precious ring disappeared into the long grass. Rose was scrambling down into the cut. When she got to the bottom she called out to one of the Wexford men and she ran and caught up with them. Michael tore at the grass. He found the ring, stuffed it inside his pocket with the box and followed her down into the cut. He was too late. He saw her wriggle through the breach in the fence and disappear behind the enormous mound that protected the nitro houses with the last of the Wexford men.

Michael plunged down an almost vertical bank onto the beach and trudged through the sand. Near the shoreline was a zigzag barrier of wooden posts and planks that ran the length of the beach. Michael clambered over the barrier and continued to the shore. He dug his heels into the hard wet sand as he walked. It helped relieve the pressure in his head and gradually his fury subsided. Still he damned Rose to hell and swore to have nothing more to do with her.

He washed his face with seawater. It cooled the bruise and his temper fell a few more degrees to the point where he was calm and he wondered if he had acted unfairly towards Rose. His mother had told him it was never right to hit a woman. But the girl had provoked him, tried to excite his jealousies when he was telling her that he loved her. It was impossible for a man to trust his own judgement when it came to women. The more he pursued her the more perplexed and frustrated he became.

Further down the beach was a soldier on patrol. Another man, a worker from the factory, was sitting not so far away on top of the zigzag barrier. After a minute or two of walking and ruminating Michael reached the man.

Good, said Michael, and he sat himself down on the barrier.

Good, said Seanee, and he raised a finger casually towards Michael's face.

Did ye get a skelp of sometin der Mick?

I mighta done, replied Michael.

And did ye skelp it back?

I did, replied Michael, except I tink I may have precipitated it meself.

Oh, I see, said Seanee, it wasn't dat wan Rose by any chance.

It might a been, said Michael.

She's more combustible dan de explosives in de factory, said Seanee.

She flares up pretty hot alright.

The soldier was passing and he tendered a cautious greeting.

How are ye goin on dere? replied Seanee, and he smiled and showed off his rotten teeth.

Fine day, said the soldier.

Not bad at all, said Michael, trying to be jovial.

Here, said Seanee, I heard dere's a whole fecken battalion of Germans over de headland.

Is that right na? said the soldier.

Not a word of a lie, said Seanee, so why don't ye go and kill a few a dem.

Go fuck yourself paddy, said the soldier.

I will sir, said Seanee obediently, I can tink of notin better I'd prefer ta do dan fuck meself.

Quit riling em will ye? said Michael.

Seanee paid no heed.

Oh, and by de way, continued Seanne, while we're on de subject of copulation, who's stickin his prick inta yer sweetheart back in England.

53

I don't care paddy, said the soldier, I've been riding your wife instead.

Very good, said Seanee, with a sly grin, you'd be doin me a considerable favour.

Give it a rest, said Michael.

Yeah, give it a bleedin rest paddy, said the soldier, and tucked his rifle strap over his shoulder and he continued on up the beach.

Don't fret yerself, said Seanee to Michael, dem lads are so bored walkin up and down dis fecken beach dey'd be glad of a bit of aggro, and he commenced laughing and coughing simultaneously.

Come on, said Michael, and both men leapt off the barrier.

Less than fifty yards from the shoreline were the huts used to dry the cordite. Each one was encircled by a low mound of sand and on each door was a number.

Murphy's supposed to be in number twenty, said Seanee, and they went from one house to the next until they found it.

Seanee mounted the one low step and knocked gingerly. The door swung outwards and Murphy came out. He was a big man and he was wearing special fireproof overalls. He was sweaty and tense. He filled his lungs with sea air, wiped his brow with a bit of cloth and looked down at Seanee.

Yer late, he said.

I am not, said Seanee, I'm bang on time, Delaney's late.

Murphy blew his swollen nose loudly into the cloth and dismissed the matter with a twitch.

Nice shiner ye got dere, he said to Michael.

Never mind dat, said Seanee, he wants a start in de dryin houses.

He does does he? said Murphy, and he began interrogating Seanee about Michael.

Another man dressed in the same fireproof overalls was inside the hut, and he took the interruption as an opportunity to take a short break until Murphy cocked his head to one side in an agitated manner and the man immediately resumed his work, and Murphy resumed questioning Seanee about Michael.

Michael caught nothing of what was being said. He was fixed entirely on the interior of the small rectangular building. It consisted of no more than a wooden floor, lead-lined walls and the most rudimentary of wooden shelves. Resting on the shelves were perforated wooden trays. Inside each tray were neat rows of cordite cylinders about four inches tall. At the far end was a small window. Below this was a large cast iron radiator. The heat from this appliance dried all the moisture from the explosive.

The man slid a tray from one of the shelves, placed it on the floor and removed the contents, one cylinder at a time, into a much larger, deeper wooden box.

I'll be back in a minute, said Murphy to the man, and he led Seanee and Michael along to the next hut.

He removed a piece of paper from inside his overalls. His thick finger raced down the left hand column and across the page. He squinted at the tiny handwritten figures, hesitated, squinted again and was satisfied that everything was in order. To the left of the door was a glass panel. Murphy wiped off the salty smudge and read the thermometer inside. He made a note on the paper with a pencil and touched the centre of the door with the flat of his hand.

You can get on with dis lot when Delaney gets here, said Murphy.

How long has de cordite been in dere? asked Seanee.

This lot, said Murphy, looking at the paper, five days, so it's good and dry.

Murphy then produced a string with keys, undid the chunky lock and pulled the door open gently.

And what about Michael? said Seanee.

It's not up ta me who works in de dryin houses, said Murphy, but I can recommend young Michael here to the foreman.

And he'll get more pay, said Seanee.

His tone was sharp and Murphy, who was clearly very tired, didn't like it.

Dat wouldn't be an unreasonable request, interjected Michael very softly.

If he gets de job, said Murphy.

If he gets de job, repeated Seanee.

Well, yer not experienced at dis work, said Murphy, when you are ye can ask for more money.

Dat's fair enough, said Michael, and Seanee assented without any further comment.

I'm gonna leave this door open, said Murphy, to let it cool down a bit more and tell Delaney dere's only brass-lined boxes in dere.

Dat's no problem at all sir, said Seanee with a little bow, and Murphy went back to the other drying house.

As soon as he was out of sight Seanee plonked down between two big clumps of grass.

Why's he checkin de temperature? asked Michael.

Dat's stuff's quare dangerous if it's not completely dry, said Seanee, and he lay back in the sand, so ye got ta handle it like a new born baby.

Are you comfortable dere? asked Michael.

I am indeedee, said Seanee, and I shall wait here until Mister Delaney arrives.

I'll see ye later, said Michael.

He got no answer, Seanee was already asleep.

Michael found the wooden walkway and headed back towards the press house. Delaney passed him on his way to the drying houses. He was annoyed at himself for being late and was shaking his head wildly. A little further on he was overtaken by

56

an empty bogey that was being pushed by a pretty young girl from his street.

Ah look, said the girl, it's lover boy.

Good, replied Michael.

How's Rose? she asked, and her eyes widened knowingly.

I wouldn't know.

Hah hah, said the girl, as if she was reading his mind, Rose doesn't keep many secrets. I've had some very vivid descriptions of what you two get up ta at lunchtime.

Michael stopped, plonked down in the sand and emptied the sand from his left boot. The girl would move on, he hoped, and let him be.

Is dat a shiner yev got dere? asked the girl.

Michael looked back towards the drying houses as if distracted by something. Delaney was kicking Seanee's feet and without warning Seanee jumped up at him like a vicious dog.

Jaysus, it is, said the girl, where did ye get dat from?

In de pub last night, said Michael.

In de pub, said the girl, last night?Yer a bloody liar.I saw ye dis mornin comin over de bridge.

Is dat right? said Micheal.

I certainly did, and I'm sure ye didn't have dat yoke on yer face, said the girl.

Michael continued watching the two men as they argued. Eventually the girl would get bored trying to rile him and would go about her business.

The brief outburst between the two men ended with some sort of grudging reconciliation and they entered the drying house together.

It wasn't Rose was it? Oh Jaysus, it was, wasn't it, she said.

The girl buried her head into her outstretched arms to hide her laughter.

Feck off will ye, said Michael.

Ah now, said the girl, sure I'm only messin with ye.

Michael yanked his other boot off and let the sand pour out.

Right so, she said, punctuating her good bye with a tut, and good luck with Rose, you're goin ta need it, and off she went on her way.

No sooner had the girl gone than Michael regretted his unkind words.

He got up to follow her and apologise but he stopped when he saw Seanee coming out the door he'd just entered. He was walking backwards and both his arms were on fire. Then the sides of the hut disintegrated into a million tiny shattered pieces. The roof had somehow remained intact. It went up, spun over and was falling again. Everywhere there were tiny glowing fragments of cotton. They burnt out almost instantly. The force of the explosion caught Michael in the chest like an enormous fist. He was lifted off his feet and was travelling backwards. Then he was on his arse in the sand. The roof came crashing down in a broken heap beside the mound. Michael heard no sound as the wooden structure came asunder. His ears were filled with a low hum and he felt the sides of his head pressing inwards. The door skimmed over him like a playing card tossed across a table. All around him were grass fires. Seanee was lying still on the sand, a charred object in the shape of a man.

CHAPTER 7

Mary stood trembling in the dark and dingy hallway of Mrs Dempsey's house. She had forgotten her key and had gone next door to find her father. She could hear him through the partly open door that led to the kitchen. He was sitting at the table drinking with his neighbour. The smell of burning tobacco drifted into the hallway. It was just one of a number of other unpleasant odours that hung about the house. Every time she entered Mary was assailed by them, and also by the bleakness and poverty of the interior. The floorboards were bare and there wasn't a rug or a mat in the entire house. The gas lamp in the hall was never lit. Mary had been up to the first floor once when Mrs Dempsey was unwell. She wasn't going up there again. The air in the tiny bedrooms was thick with the musty scent of stale human breath and flesh, and the wallpaper in every room had been destroyed by her seven children who ran in and out of the front door shouting and screaming like animals from morning to night.

But the real cause of her uncontrolled shaking was the soldier with the blond hair and what he'd done to her. He'd appeared unannounced at the kitchen window of the doctor's house with the neighbour's dog cradled unwillingly in his arms. He was down by the beach, said the soldier, through the glass, and he let himself in through the back door. He let the animal fall to the ground and it sat by Mary's feet growling at him.

Dat's not our dog, Mary explained.

The soldier grabbed it by the collar and put it outside. She could see another soldier through the far window. He was in the front garden.

The blond haired soldier raised his eyebrows. You're trapped now, he was saying, and I can do what I want with you.

Mary stepped backwards into the living room. She wanted to call out but all the breath had gone out of her body.

He pulled her back with one violent tug and pushed her up against the pantry door. If only Thomas had done it to her, she would have submitted to him willingly, not to this soldier. His hands were on her breasts and her buttocks. He pressed his mouth onto hers. His breath stank of fags and strong alcohol. She opened her mouth to bite him. He drew back and pulled up her dress. He found the nakedness beneath and his rough fingers were forcing themselves between her thighs. She lashed out with a fist to his face and he stopped. His accomplice was knocking on the window. He was banging so hard the sash rattled in the window frame. A motorcar was coming up the hill. The engine was roaring with the effort of the steep incline. The soldier let Mary go. He was suddenly sober. He looked as if he'd just woken from a dream.

Get out, said Mary, and he left.

Standing in her neighbour's hall she could still feel his stubble on her cheek and his cold clammy fingers squeezing into her skin, and she could smell his tunic, damp from the rain.

A noise in Mrs Dempsey's kitchen made her start. Her father had knocked over a glass and was apologising repeatedly. She was about to enter to get the key and be gone when her mother's name was mentioned. Like a mouse, Mary moved a little closer.

I'm so stupid, said her father.

Ah sure it's only a glass darlin, said Mrs Dempsey, if it was de whole bottle, well dat would be a different story altogether.

I'm a bag a nerves, he said.

60

Yer still gettin over yer wife's death dat's all, said Mrs Dempsey.

Hah, he said, she's de cause of it, she made me like dis long before she died.

I do remember ye sayin as much, said his neighbour, implying politely that she'd heard it before and she didn't wish to hear it again.

She made me feel worse dan useless, he said.

Ye should view her passing as a new start, she Mrs Dempsey, in an attempt to steer him away from the subject he'd been boring her with ever since his wife's funeral. It was partly her own fault. She had indulged him at first. She'd derived considerable pleasure from hearing the 'great woman' being taken down a peg or two by her husband. In the end she had paid one hundred fold for the pleasure, and the tasty morsels she had chewed on and digested were now being fed to her every other day. And she noted with considerable irony that the way he spoke of his wife was enough to convict him of the very crimes and shortcomings his wife had accused him of.

Notin, he said, near to shouting, notin was good enough for her.

She was a hard woman alright, added the neighbour.

Notin, he repeated, with a sob, notin was ever right for her.

These particular words, once uttered, were a sure sign to Mrs Dempsey that he was on a fixed course and nothing would derail him except earthquake or fire.

It must have been awful for ye, said Mrs Dempsey, with a long sigh of resignation, and she poured herself another glass of poitin.

She was a perfectionist, he said, and an awful domineerin woman, she took away all a me confidence.

How did ye cope? said Mrs Dempsey, as she puffed on a wrinkled fag and wondered what to have for dinner.

61

With dis stuff, he said, and he poked his glass.

Well she's not comin back, said Mrs Dempsey.

What? he asked impatiently.

She's not comin back, repeated Mrs Dempsey, in a more sympathetic way.

No, she's not, he said glumly, and God will punish me for being such a bad fader.

Yer in good company den, she said, he'll be no kinder ta me, and she poured him yet another drink.

And me poor daughter, she never-

Mary didn't catch the rest of what was said, the front door burst open and four children ran inside yelling as loud as their lungs would permit. The kitchen door was next to be assaulted and it collided with the press causing the few bits of Delph the woman possessed to rattle, and the children ran around the table with no apparent purpose other than to pester the two adults sitting there.

Her brother was out on the street with the *Wicklow People* stuffed tightly under his arm. The remainder of the Dempsey tribe, two boys and a girl, had taken hold of his grubby jacket and were demanding money. Michael threw a coin high up into the air and they scrambled down the footpath after it, elbowing and shoving each other greedily. Michael took his chance to escape and Mary followed him inside their house. He lay the paper on the table and began tending to the fire in the front room. No words passed between them. He had gone to the hospital several times to see Seanee and on each occasion he'd returned home despondent. Now he passed his evenings staring and spitting into the fire and wondering, why Seanee and not me. Mary would've been grateful if providence had been so kind to her in such circumstances. Michael however considered himself a sort of cheat who had evaded his true fate at the price of his friend. And there was no talking to him. He had settled into his gloom and no reasoning would shake him out of it.

Mary had hoped that the dark mood that had enveloped him since the accident would lift and they would be able to speak, not only for his sake, but for her own. It hadn't. If anything he had withdrawn even further into himself and when she opened her mouth to speak she was given his back. So she went to the kitchen, made some tea and opened the stove to light the fire. The coal was falling from her shaking hands and she could barely hold the match steady enough to light the paper. Behind her, on a high shelf, stood her father's poitín. A little drop might do her some good, she thought, and put her right for the time being at least. It wouldn't be like drinking, it was medicinal, to help her with the shock. That's what was making her so silly, the shock. In a day or two she'd have forgotten about the whole thing. The soldier was drunk and got excited the way way men sometimes did, it was nothing to make a big fuss about.

Her eyes and cheeks were red and wet from crying. She wiped them in her apron, quietly uncorked the bottle, poured a good measure into her teacup and replaced the bottle exactly where it had been.

Her father returned soon afterwards and the door was slammed shut. He came into the kitchen and grunted a salutation to which Mary, due to the strong effects of the alcohol, was unable to reply.

He took the bottle from the shelf, rubbed his chin and put it back again.

Ah, he said, I've had enough of dat for one day, and he went sullenly back into the front room.

What's eightin ye, said Michael.

My dissolute life, replied his father.

What are ye talkin about? said Michael.

63

Never mind, said his father, picking up the *Wicklow People*, and he sat in his chair by the hearth and unfolded the paper to read the article on the front page.

He mumbled through the first three paragraphs.

Read it out loud or don't read it all, said Michael.

Cool your boilers lad, said his father, I'm lookin for the important bit, and then he raised his index finger.

Here it is, he continued, and he commenced reading in his best oratorical voice.

The *Wicklow People* was yesterday told that a preliminary report written by Colonel A. Ford, the Inspector of Explosives has been sent to the Secretary of State. In his report the Colonel said that two very important facts came to light in the course of his inquiry regarding the recent explosion at the Kynoch factory in Arklow. Firstly, nine days before the explosion, while a charge of nitroglycerine was being run down into a covered channel an empty bottle was also carried down and fell with a splash into a vat below. If it had fallen on the bottom with the first portion of the nitroglycerine it would scarcely have failed to cause an explosion and probably the loss of five lives.

Well be-de-hookey, he exclaimed.

The bottle could only have been placed in the channel with some difficulty and the Colonel concluded that it was not put there with a view to concealment as it might have been effectively hidden behind the channel or in gorse bushes growing nearby.

What do ye make a dat now? said his father.

What's dat got ta do with what happened to Seanee and Delaney? asked Michael.

The implication I believe, said his father, is dat the explosion was caused deliberately by one of yer fellow workers.

And why would dey do dat? asked Michael.

64

Lord bless us and save us, said his father, yer mother was right all along, the chap's dumbfounded.

I asked ye a question, said Michael.

To get more money a course, said his father, in a long drawnout drawl, isn't dat what half de men are after?

Mary continued listening from the kitchen while she sipped her tea. She felt strange inside. The initial burning and irritation in her stomach had passed after a few minutes and she was left with a warmth all over as if she was wrapped in a thick blanket. She had even forgotten about the pain in her back and her feet and by the time the dinner had been prepared, unbeknownst to her, she was drunk.

She brought the food for all three of them into the front room and they all sat down together to eat.

Are ye alright dere girl? asked her father.

Yes, said Mary, trying to disguise her alarm, do I not look alright?

Ye look like yev had a few drops of de auld crater, observed her father.

If anybody would know, he would, said Michael.

Yer face is flushed, said her father, and yer manners are bit peculiar now.

The mere suspicion that she had been drinking mortified her. She had spoken so disapprovingly of it in the past, to be caught drunk would make her a terrible hypocrite. Fortunately for Mary little else was said over the meal and after Michael had finished he went into his room. When he came out he'd changed into his good suit and boots.

Jaysus, said his father, de shine on dem 'ed take eye de out a ye.

Off ta see some female no doubt, said Mary.

Delaney's funeral is at seven, said Michael.

Mary and her father shrunk in shame.

Can ye believe dat? said her father, with all dat's been going on I forgot about dat poor auld Delaney fella, God rest his soul.

And by de way, said Michael quietly, as he tidied himself in front of the mirror above the mantelpiece, I saw yer sweetheart today.

I don't have any sweetheart, said Mary, and she picked up the pile of dirty dishes, including her own plate of half-eaten food.

Well whatever you refer to dat Thomas chap, said Michael.

Mary felt the ground beneath her tilting. She set the dishes back on the table.

Where did ye see him? she asked, steadying herself on the back of a chair.

What difference does it make where I met him, said Michael, he'll be at de mass.

Why didn't you tell me earlier? asked Mary.

I had other tings on me mind, he explained plainly, and he took his cap from the hook on the back of the door and left.

CHAPTER 8

The pubs were jammed all along the Main Street with men spending the wages they had just received. They poured out onto the road and stood in the rain in their work clothes clutching their pints. It was just as his mother had predicted. The publicans, she said, they were the ones who would really profit from the factory. Some of the men called to Michael drunkenly. They wanted to buy him a drink. His name had become well known after the accident and they were keen to hear his account of the explosion. They considered him some kind of hero. Michael paid no heed to any of it. He waved the men off and went on his way.

He passed his mother's empty shop and went through the gates of the church, mounted the steps and went as he and his family always did not to the main entrance, but to the small chapel to the left of the main altar. He stopped in a corner by the porch where the rain wasn't falling and joined a small huddle of men who were all smoking. Michael did as all the others did. He lit his cigarette and held it respectfully behind his back. As the men chatted a young priest came strutting out of the sacristy and opened an umbrella. In his other hand was a fat bible.

Jaysus lads, watch out, said one of the men, here comes dat young pup.

How is a man so lackin in years supposed ta have any real wisdom ta impart? asked another, with a mystified shake of his head.

He's too well bred ta understand de people of dis town, said a third, and with that they all went scurrying like children into the church leaving Michael, who'd only just begun his cigarette, to engage with the priest.

The young man shoved his shiny new bible into his broad belt, offered Michael his soft palm, squeezed his arm and said hello in his genteel accent.

He was tall and thin and wore glasses, and he reminded Michael of the boys who were always bullied at school.

How's it goin Fader? said Michael, and he looked down at his own feet. He had no idea of what to say beyond this.

Yer named after de archangel Michael, said the novice priest.

So I am, said Michael.

And ye know what an archangel is? asked the priest.

A special angel, said Michael.

And when ye think upon yer recent misfortunes, said the priest, ye should remember dat he was endowed with great courage.

Michael swung his arm from behind his back and took a long, heavy drag on the cigarette.

Is dat right Fader? he said, raising his head slowly, and he stared into the soft, stupid eyes of the innocent priest. Then he looked away.

The bell was ringing out the hour of seven and his sister was rushing up the steps with a scarf wrapped around her head. She passed Michael and they exchanged no more than a glance.

Michael turned again to the priest, tilted his head, closed his left eye, and pushed his hat up by the brim.

Why should I remember dat in particular Fader?

Well Michael, said the priest, with a nervous cough, you may have been given some of that courage too.

Michael let the cigarette fall to the ground and he pressed the toe of his boot down on it as if he was trying to extinguish the life of a horrible insect.

68

I'll bear dat in mind Fader, he said, and he followed his sister into the church.

Mary pressed her way through a dozen or so people that were crammed tightly together at the bottom of the aisle. She spied a spot at the end of a pew where she could just about fit. She squeezed her slender body in the tiny space and sat. She felt most peculiar and unsettled. The atmosphere was oppressive. The enormous radiators were blasting out a great heat and a mist of steam was rising up off the damp clothing of the congregation. Mary removed her scarf and coat to stop her from fainting. The poitin that had numbed her earlier was wearing off, leaving her in an even worse state than she had been before she'd taken it. Her head was throbbing, her mouth was dry and she thought she might be sick.

Kneeling before the coffin was the wife and mother of the dead man. They were sobbing uncontrollably, their eyes running with tears and it seemed as though they would never stop. But the only thing Mary could think about, apart from her terrible condition, was Thomas. She thought herself selfish to think of him while a man lay there in a coffin. But she couldn't help herself and she searched the centre of the church where he and his brother usually sat and when she didn't see either of them she went into a kind of panic. She closed her eyes and listened to her breathing, like her mother had taught her to do as a child. She opened them after a couple of minutes and gradually her nerves began to settle.

The parish priest stood at the altar. His name was Father Dunphy and he could not have been more different from the priest Michael had encountered outside. He was no more than five and a half feet tall with a barrel chest and broad shoulders that filled every inch of his cassock and he was well advanced in years. Short as he was, he was a most imposing figure, wrought

69

not by his collar and the office conferred upon him but by his own strength of character and personality.

After reading from the gospels he withdrew from the ornate lectern and ascended the pulpit. He spoke unhurriedly, his words falling with great weight upon the congregation. He spoke of the tragedy of John Delaney's death and he complained about the company's accusations of sabotage. There was a chorus of agreement and a few of the more expressive in the congregation cursed the factory owner. The parish priest hushed them down with a single resolute gesture and he continued. Our complaint will be made in a rational manner, he said, at the meeting in the courthouse at eight this evening.

The entire congregation was under his spell, all except Mary. She brooded upon Thomas and how quickly the wall she had built in her mind between them had crumbled. She remembered her earlier determination, her promise to herself that she would forget all about him and here she was, running after him like a silly little girl. And why had he not sought her out? He knew where to find her. And what would she say to him when she did eventually find him? Too much kindness was a sign of weakness, and equally if she was too cold she would drive him away. What she really wanted was to do was to scream at him, tell him he was a fool for leaving her, and when all the resentment was out of her and he had begged her forgiveness she would give in to him and allow him to put his arms around her.

The sermon finished and the ceremony dragged on from one Latin prayer and refrain to the next. Mary's only prayer was for it all to end. The heat was suffocating her. She wanted the cold fresh air and rain on her face and as soon as communion began she left and went and waited by the gate in the pitiful drizzle. The entrance was so narrow she was bound to see Thomas. And then, after ten long minutes, a mass of bodies emerged and came rushing down the steps as if driven on by flood waters, everyone

70

of them determined to get a good seat at the meeting in the court house opposite. They passed her in a blur that soon became a mere trickle of the aged stooping and hobbling. Still she remained steadfastly at her self-appointed post until the very last had departed and only then did she return to the church to see if Thomas had lingered for some reason. Apart from a few mourners by the coffin the place was strangely silent, the pews deserted, the people gone.

Mary genuflected, blessed herself with holy water and left. Perhaps he had gone to the meeting. So, wet and miserable, she followed the train of men and women and children across the road. Again she was confronted by a large crowd. The modestly sized building wasn't nearly big enough to contain them all. The entrance was mobbed and there was no way to get beyond them. She went to the east side of the courthouse. She thought she might be able to see through one of the large windows. She found many people gathered around them, all craning and contorting for the tiniest bit of a view or a chance to catch what was being said within. On the west side was the same arrangement of windows affording the same view, most however were deterred as the way was blocked by trees and a tangle of thorny bushes, except for a few children who braved the thicket and were hoisting one another up to a window. Mary yanked up her dress to the knees and followed them through the briars and brambles. Her headscarf was caught by the merciless, grabbing thorns and she left it there. Once she had penetrated the first few feet the overgrowth became much thinner and an uneven path of mud emerged. She slid and stumbled past the boys to an open window a little further along. The ground rose up and she found herself peering over the heads of the people packed inside the tiny hall.

At the far end, on a low makeshift stage of loose planks and crates, were three men seated on flimsy chairs. Mary recognised only one, Father Dunphy, who sat with his arms folded tightly around his stout body as if he were holding in some force that was trying to get out and consequently was causing his solid bulk to swell even more than usual.

A fourth man with an elaborate moustache and a fine gold watch chain was standing and reading a speech from some rough notes he held in his shaky grasp. His audience was equally restless. Everywhere she looked Mary saw angry and distraught faces. There was a simmering fury at what the man was saying. He proceeded with caution and seemed to lack the courage to give full vent to the stern words he had penned in the solitude where he no doubt he had felt himself considerably more daring than he truly was.

He pulled at his dainty whiskers and toyed with his expensive watch chain.

...vast sums of money have been spent on the construction of this factory, the man said, and we have brought much-needed employment, and yet advantage has been taken of the tragedy that has recently occurred.

Father Dunphy leaned forward in his chair to interject.

The people of Arklow have always been very grateful to Mister Chamberlain, said the priest, for introducing to our neighbourhood an industry that is giving a livelihood to so many...

The man raised his papers in protest.

Even so, he said, the company would prefer to close the works forever rather than be forced to yield to unjust demands, and he turned to the austere gentleman to his left. The gentleman's eyes closed and his head fell in assent.

The tension was rising like a steady swell throughout the hall and was threatening to erupt into bloody turmoil.

The austere gentleman drew himself up and the other relinquished the stage. He was a good six foot in height, gaunt and well attired in a frock coat and patent leather shoes. Mary

72

guessed him to be, by his air of superiority, the owner. He had the pallor of a corpse and by his icy delivery it was clear to all present that he assumed that an attitude of deference should and would be accorded him.

You may grumble, he said, however, as you are all well aware, we pay the highest wages in the district and the men are employed partly from a feeling of consideration towards the district and the hope of educating you into good workmen...

A warm current of air was wafting out through the window caressing Mary's cheeks. Chamberlain's words were drifting away and for a tiny instant she imagined wind and waves carrying her off. But her feet were cold. She looked down. She was standing in a shallow puddle and her dress was muddied and torn at the hem. The only blessing was the canopy of leaves and branches that sheltered her from the relentless drizzle.

...and we have seen carelessness and disobedience to the rules...

Indignation rippled through the room. Mary was oblivious to it all. She searched for Thomas' shiny black hair, his slender features and his slight stoop amongst the crowd. Here and there were young men who appeared very much like him. They were cousins and nephews of the same clan. And each time she caught sight of one of these relatives she thought for an instant she had found him and then her heart sank in her chest with cruel disappointment.

...now we have possible sabotage, demands for more money and evidence that strikers have been assaulting other men who are happy to work...

The parish priest could restrain his fury no more. He threw himself forward and confronted the much taller man.

I cannot stand by and hear such gross slander of my people, he said. Regarding the explosion, there is no evidence of malice. In the case of the bottle that was found in the vat and the

73

behaviour of some of the strikers I would say this, I said to you at the outset of this enterprise that great care should be taken in the selection of men to fill positions of danger and trust in the factory. I am sorry that my advice was not taken.

A roar of wild applause burst forth. Chamberlain remained stony and unmoved. A third man in a stiff military uniform now took the centre stage. He removed his cap, placed it on his chair and began to read from a cheaply printed handbill.

It is no secret, he said, that the Kynoch Works is engaged in carrying out important government contracts and it has been brought to our attention by Mister Cocking that, because of the indiscriminate issuing of liquor to the employees of the company by licensed houses in Arklow, that working capacity has suffered and reduced the ability of the factory to fulfil its obligations. Therefore I am hereby restricting the opening hours of public houses in the urban district of Arklow from noon to two in the afternoon and from five in the afternoon to ten at night. This will take effect from tonight.

The crowd exploded at this revelation. The few that had been seated leapt up like a current of electricity had been shot through them. There was shock and disbelief at what was being said. Even the more placid let loose their venom at what they saw as an unjustifiable infringement of their God-given right to drink. They clenched their fists and taunted the men on the stage with threats and foul abuse. The priest tried in vain to calm his flock while Chamberlain and the other two men climbed down from the stage and marched in single file to the safety of a back room that was guarded by an armed soldier.

CHAPTER 9

The storm of words was over and the people of Arklow had had enough of God and death and the managers of the factory. And the men wanted a drink. They would discuss their outrage in the comfort of the pub and out they marched into the rain, each to his favourite watering hole. And there were plenty to choose from. The Main Street had seventeen pubs from which the men could make a selection, from the grandeur of the Royal Hotel to grubby shebeens, and everything in between. It was in one of these establishments that Mary thought she might find Thomas. Still, it seemed hopeless. The drizzle had turned to a torrent and the men had moved in off the street. There was not one person to ask of his whereabouts and she hadn't the courage to go into any of the pubs alone.

She walked down the Main Street in the downpour, her hair falling in long, lank strands over her face. So this is how it would be to be destitute, she thought, to be alone in a city with no friend to turn to. Was this what she was wishing for? Scattered on the ground were the printed handbills the army officer had read from in the courthouse. Mary found one in a doorway. Somehow it had escaped the deluge. Mary picked it up. Across the top in bold letters it said *THE DEFENSE OF THE REALM* and below was a military insignia. Mary spat on it, crumpled it into a ball and threw it back where she found it.

She continued walking - for no reason she herself could determine - in the direction of the Lower Main Street. At the post office she saw the figure of a woman staggering towards her.

Mary studied her cautiously as she approached. Her upper body was leaning forward at a very peculiar angle as if she was chasing after something and her arms swung about with no apparent control. It was her neighbour Mrs Dempsey.

The woman took a moment to focus on the person before her and then she said Mary's name as if she had met a long lost friend.

Yer mouldy, said Mary.

I am not, declared the woman, and she staggered backwards.

You are so, she said, ye can barely hould yerself up.

Never mind me, she said.

And who's lookin after yer children? Mary asked reproachfully.

Why me dutiful husband a course, said Mrs Dempsey smugly, who else, so dere's no need to worry like. I told em I was just goin ta de shop and I taut I might have a quick one or two while I was out.

Go home ta bed for God's sake, said Mary.

And what about you me poor darlin? Yer all wet and dirty, she said, don't ye have a scarf?

Mary touched her hair. She'd forgotten she had been wearing it when she left the house. She was about to explain how it had been lost and she thought better of it. Her neighbour was already moving onto another more pressing matter.

Do ye have a spare shillin? she asked in a slur.

No, said Mary, and she asked her neighbour if she had seen Thomas.

I mighta done, she said, with a sly grin.

Well did ye or didn't ye? asked Mary.

It so happens dat I did, said Mrs Dempsey, and her twisted tongue darted out of the corner of her mouth.

Where? demanded Mary.

Jaysus, said Mrs Dempsey, rubbing her chin, if only I could remember.

My God, said Mary, yer pitiful, and she removed her worn leather purse from the pocket in her dress. She was close to crying. Her neighbour let it go by. She was blind to her distress. Her concerns lay only in the contents of Mary's purse.

Mary snapped open the rusty metal clasp and was counting the pennies. Her neighbour shot a glance inside and with a lightning swoop that amazed Mary she grabbed the purse.

Have ye lost yer mind? said Mary.

The woman clutched it to her breast out of Mary's reach and emptied most of the contents into her greedy hand.

Is dat all yev got? she said, I taut ye got yer wages yesterday.

The woman's eyes were wild and burning and she was half crazy from the alcohol.

She didn't pay me, said Mary.

Her neighbour blinked.

A likely story, she said, probably hidden under yer bed, and she returned the purse with the few remaining pennies.

Where is he? asked Mary.

Are ye sure ye want to know? said her neighbour, ye may not like what ye find.

Mary pushed the hair from her face and repeated the question.

I saw him in The Harbour Bar, said Mrs Dempsey, no place for a woman dat.

Good enough for you though, said Mary.

It would be a grand spot if it wasn't rammed full of arseholes from Wexford, said her neighbour, jingling the coins, and off she went up the street attempting to whistle a popular tune.

Mary skulked along the footpath close to the shop fronts. Constables and soldiers were coming up the street. They were going from pub to pub warning the customers to be out by ten. In every place they were greeted by the most tremendous hullabaloo

77

and jeering. The sight of their rifles caused a deepening chill in Mary's already cold body. They passed her without comment. They were tense and purposeful. Mary avoided their glances. She feared the blond haired soldier was among them, but they all wore oilskin ponchos with large hoods and in the fading light she couldn't tell one from another.

She continued on down to the Lower Main Street. The bar was the only public house in this part of the town, and the music and laughter and general rowdiness emanating from it seemed all the more raucous because of the silence that surrounded it. Mary was too frightened to enter. She found an empty beer crate by the door and flipped it upside-down. From her little platform she had a clear view through the window into the three rooms that made up the bar. It was much as she had imagined it would be. A small turf fire burnt in the hearth. Cigarette and pipe smoke hung like an eerie mist above the men's heads. A quartet of musicians sat around a small table in the poky room at the rear of the bar. Every square inch of the table before the musicians was occupied with glasses, most of them empty. It was the same throughout the bar - there wasn't space enough to rest an elbow. And the booze had clearly got the better of the musicians. They sang off-key and struggled to bring forth the correct notes from their instruments. It mattered little, no one was listening. The rest of the rabble was engaged in getting served or shouting at each other. The only real purpose of the quartet was to make it necessary for everyone to raise their voices to be heard.

In the middle of all this was Thomas. Mary caught sight of him almost immediately. He was perched on a stool looking down on a number of other young men who stood in a tight circle around him. He appeared to be amusing them with a story. Mary guessed he was relating one of his adventures at sea. But there was an uneasiness in his companions. The cause was plain to see. It was the workers from Wexford seated in the corner. Copious

78

amounts of stout had made them brazen and hostile and some very rough exchanges were being passed between them and Thomas' friends.

Mary knocked frantically on the glass. She was desperate to get Thomas' attention before a terrible brawl broke out. The only response was from a few customers near the window who waved at her playfully. She had no choice, if she wanted to see him she would have to enter the pub. She pushed the door open and came face-to-face with the unruly mob. The noise was deafening, it was as hot as an oven and there was broken glass underfoot. A good proportion of the customers were very young, mere boys Mary thought. Three of these youths were slumped in a heap in the back room, probably put there out of harm's way. Those directly in front of Mary stopped their talking and drinking. They were momentarily fixed by this vision of the bedraggled figure, and they had no notion of her intentions. They took her for a beggar woman in search of money until she pointed in Thomas' general direction and they made way for her, watching her as they would some spectre, as she passed.

A lull in the music announced her arrival at the counter and the circle around Thomas was broken so all could see the spectacle of a woman in The Harbour Bar. She looked straight at him. He seemed different. His brief time at sea had obviously brought about a change in him. The suit he wore was brand new and his unkempt hair was tamed with some kind of fancy oil or grease. The boy in him was gone, she thought and had been replaced by something which wasn't quite a man. And there was no smile, no gesture of affection to greet her. He was neither surprised nor disappointed at seeing her. The only thing she detected was mild embarrassment, nothing more, and if they had not known otherwise his companions could have easily mistaken her for an absolute stranger.

Thomas laid his pint down, climbed off his stool and his friends moved ominously up along the counter to allow the pair to speak in private. Mary saw her reflection in the mirror behind the bar and was horrified. She was humiliating herself. It was bad enough that she had come to search him out. It would have been far wiser to have stayed at home. He would have come in his own good time, if he'd wanted to come at all and then the meeting would have been on her terms. And to have come to this place in such a terrible condition, she would never forgive herself for it, never.

Eventually she spoke. She asked Thomas to go outside, to get away from the terrible din. But the words she uttered were inaudible, even to her. The musicians had resumed their work with even greater gusto than before and the slagging match between Thomas' friends and the Wexford men was becoming louder and more venomous. Somewhere behind her a glass smashed. The owner and his wife let out a simultaneous roar of vexation and he declared with a wild sweep of his arm that no more drink would be served. Thomas kept staring into the corner. He and his companions were simmering with rage and intent on settling matters outside with their fists. Mary couldn't bear it. She turned swiftly and jostled her way out of the awful place back out into the cold and rain.

Thomas followed her begrudgingly, passing two police constables as he stepped out onto the street. They were already bellowing orders for the men to leave without delay.

Mary was skulking along the footpath. Thomas overtook her easily and he blocked her path. Her eyes were swollen with tears and her nose was pouring with snot. She wiped it away roughly with her sleeve.

I see yev acquired a taste for alcohol, she said.

The company of seamen is no place for abstinence, he replied.

And I suppose yev indulged in a few other pleasures besides, said Mary.

Havin a few pints is one ting, said Thomas, what yer referrin ta would be another matter altogether.

And what does dat mean? asked Mary.

She was upset when she heard herself say the words, she hadn't set out to argue with him and now she was accusing him of lustful acts with no evidence.

De meanin is plain enough, replied Thomas.

Well ye haven't been savin yerself for me, said Mary, ye never even came ta visit me.

And ye never answered me letter, said Thomas.

Where was I to send it? asked Mary snivelling.

If yed a bothered to read it ye would've seen an address in Woolwich, said Thomas, clearly ye didn't.

What's dat above yer eye, said Mary, and she reached out to touch a deep purple scar above his left eyebrow.

Don't change de subject, he said, brushing her away.

I didn't tink ye were ever comin back, she said.

Thomas was rigid, determined to suppress his emotions.

Look at me, she said feebly, I've been wanderin around tryin ta find ye all night.

I was goin ta go and see ye tomorrow, he said.

I'm completely drenched, she said, tugging at her dress. If a drop of rain had touched my head before ye would've given me yer jacket.

Tings have changed, he said.

Why? she demanded, why have dey changed?

When ye didn't answer me letter I taut ye didn't want me anymore.

I do, she said, and she pressed her open hands to his chest, I do.

But Thomas wasn't listening.

...and den I started tinking, he said, and I realised dat I wasn't ready ta settle down.

Ye said yed come back for me, she said, instead ye left me here to dese savages. Ye had tasted de freedom, de freedom I wanted so much and ye were so afraid of and now ye won't give it up.

Dat's about the size it, said Thomas.

And ye'll be off again in no time, she said, and won't be back for God knows how long.

I'm goin ta Woolwich, I'll be back in no time.

And will ye come and see me?

Thomas didn't have a chance to reply. The dispute inside the bar had descended into a riot. Furniture was being thrown about. The music stopped and there was screaming and yelling. A stool was hurled through the front window. It landed on the road and the men came after, falling through the door with their fists and boots swinging in every direction. About twenty in all were laying into each other. The police constables were blowing their whistles and waving their sticks menacingly. Give it up lads, give it up, they were shouting. It did little to deter the brawlers. Both sides were out for blood, and broken bones. One Arklow man was receiving the brunt of the Wexford men's attention. He was beaten to the ground and he curled up into a ball with his arms around his head for protection while he was kicked and punched viciously.

It's Michael, said Thomas.

Mary let out a demented scream and begged the men to stop.

Soldiers came tearing down the Main Street. Behind them were mounted horses. The Wexford men began to scatter. Most of them headed down the street towards the harbour. More soldiers came running at them from this direction and they turned in the hope of getting past the horses.

The horsemen advanced towards them at a canter with batons drawn. An empty bottle was hurled, hitting one of the horsemen and the animal skidded on the wet cobblestone. The other horseman pulled hard on his reins to avoid a collision and the beast rose up on its hind legs. Mary saw the hooves of the snorting horse about to descend upon her and she fainted in terror.

CHAPTER 10

The workers came up the hill and along the road. Oscar passed small groups walking and talking together. He was used to seeing them. He saw them every day on his many aimless wanderings around the town. Their numbers swelled as he neared the barracks, their flat caps bobbing up and down, arms swinging in grey and black suits, waistcoats, white shirts and boots. There were so many it was impossible to progress down the hill. Fortunately he was early for his appointment so he stepped into the ditch and lit a cigarette.

Opposite was the doctor's house. He considered going to the door and knocking. He tried to imagine the scene. It was a kind of mental dress rehearsal, a preparation for the inevitable confrontation. His usual method for ending affairs was to disappear, to become aloof, or hide away, and not answer the telephone. That was in London, here it would be much more difficult. The town was too small. There was no escape from her really. And she would not give him up so easily, nor did he really wish her to.

And yet the thought of her made him quite angry. Their association had been intended as a bit of amusement, a way to pass the long dull evenings in a place they had both been transplanted, she by her husband, he by his profligate father. It was a relationship forged largely out of this common complaint, a mutual dislike for the town where they both found themselves, nothing more. He wasn't looking for love, he was too vain for that. If he wanted to get ahead in life he believed it was best to keep himself free. He had so few of his own resources to draw upon, to add another weight would be unwise. It was only the weakness of boredom that had drawn him to her. Otherwise he would have easily resisted the temptation of growing ever closer to her to the point that the inevitable separation would cause them both troubles.

The crowd was thinning so he resumed his walking. He passed the hospital, with the tall trees and the community of crows, and down the hill, swung onto the north quay and stopped at the entrance to the factory. He looked at his watch. He was precisely on time. Punctuality was not a quality he had required in the past and he was disappointed at how quickly he was adjusting to his new circumstances as a common worker.

He stepped over to the quay wall and peered down into the Avoca River. Sticking out of the stonework was a pipe about three feet in diameter. Waste poured out of its gaping mouth into the shallow waters. The sludge formed a dark brown pool and the current was too weak to take it away, so there it stayed, growing like a pus-filled abscess. He pitied the river, like he pitied the men. He pitied their dirty clothes and their lives that were nothing except drinking and drudgery. At least they had refused to be conscripted. They weren't stupid enough for that, unlike the English. He remembered the soldiers in London at the beginning of the war and their jubilant roars and chanting as they went off for the front. They thought they were on some great adventure, or off to fighting for some great ideal. They weren't jubilant any more. They weren't talking about freedom or the bloody king and the bloody country any more.

Oscar stared at the water. He had never seen a fish or a plant in it. The waste was pumped out of the factory day and night, and the poison made it impossible for the river to support life. Even more filth flowed into the river from the mines. Oscar had sampled the water at the village of Avoca. It tasted of copper and it dried instantly on the tongue. The sky above fared little better.

It was a clear still day and without the interference of the wind the full extent of foulness that was being expelled from the numerous chimneys could be seen. Great volumes of smoke ascended upwards towards its celestial destination. Oscar pictured the saints and cherubs coughing and heaven's pristine whiteness soiled by a dirty black smog.

And what awaited him inside this dreadful place? A dreary office and a desk he would be compelled to sit at eight or ten hours a day. The prospect terrified him. He had never worked a day in his life. His father's inherited fortune had afforded him the opportunity of acquiring the habits and manners of that class unburdened by work. It was a burden he was going to have to learn to carry. His father had squandered the money in spectacular fashion, leaving Oscar to earn his living. And what earthly function could he perform in such a place, or any other place of employment? He had been trained in the art of hedonism and practiced it with such enthusiasm that any other way of life seemed utterly unimaginable.

He consulted his watch again. Twenty minutes had passed since his arrival. He was not used to waiting for other people and it irritated him immensely. Still, he hoped Cocking wouldn't come. If he failed to keep his promise of finding him a suitable position it would be far better. But he would come eventually. He was delayed or maybe he had forgotten. Whatever the reason, it wasn't the end of it. Oscar weighed his position. He had done his bit by arriving at the agreed time and waiting as long as politeness required, so he would leave a message with one of the factory guards. If his leaving provoked Cocking into reneging on his promise, all the better, it suited Oscar perfectly well.

He went into the guard's hut to the left of the entrance. A police constable and a guard were in a cubicle off to the side. They were playing cards for money. Oscar cleared his throat loudly. Now the decision was made he wanted to be gone quickly. It would be awkward to meet Cocking as he left.

The guard, an enormous man, came out and laid his giant hands casually on the counter.

I was supposed to meet Mister Cocking here about thirty minutes ago, said Oscar, he seems ta have been held up somewhere.

The guard made a sucking noise through his teeth and he presented Oscar with his huge open palms.

I'd have no idea of de General Manager's comings and goings, said the giant.

Dat's quite understandable, said Oscar, with a little laugh to disguise his annoyance, can I write him a note?

A course ye can sir, a course ye can, said the guard, and he reached out one of his long arms, picked up a pencil from the end of the counter and placed it daintily in front of Oscar.

Now, continued the guard, with a tiny worried gasp, a piece a paper, a piece a paper, ye'd tink we'd have plenty a paper in here. We've log books galore, logs for every damn ting under de sun, and nare a bit a paper, can ye believe dat?

Oscar leaned on the counter and looked out the door to see if Cocking's car was coming. A few women were by the entrance. They had lingered there at the end of their shift to gossip. Another young woman, dressed in a tidy frock - obviously not a factory worker - was asking the women something. Her pretty face was familiar to Oscar. It was Mary. She was making some urgent enquiry to which the women had no information.

Dere ye go!

The constable had come out of the cubicle and without even looking laid his hands on a blank sheet of paper.

Come on will ye, he said to the gentle giant, I want a chance ta win back a few pennies before ye go home.

Oscar chewed on the end of the pencil while he composed a message in his head. He had just finished his scribbling when the giant got to his feet once again and the constable was huffing and puffing.

Mary was at the steps of the hut.

What can I do for ye Mary?

Have ye seen Thomas? she said.

No, I can't say dat I have, was the guard's soft reply.

Oscar handed the note to the constable and waved a greeting to Mary.

Hello sir, she replied, and she told the guard she was just going to see if he was on one of the ships moored at the quay.

No, no, no, said the guard, ye can't do dat Mary.

Why not? she asked.

Ye don't work here anymore, he explained calmly, and if yer not an employee or here on official business I-

Ah please John, she interrupted, I only want ta go down de quay.

Ye just can't, said the guard, and de big boss man 'll be here any minute.

Well one of ye can come with me, she said.

We can't do dat either, said the guard solemnly, ever since de explosion we've been instructed ta stay at de gates.

Next Mary suggested getting one of the girls to accompany her, and she spun around to call one of them, but they had departed and were in the middle of the bridge.

Mary began rubbing her hands together anxiously.

Can't you take me in sir? she said to Oscar.

He doesn't work here, said the guard.

He's friend's with de General Manager, aren't ye sir? said Mary.

Oscar hesitated. If he went with her there would be no chance of avoiding Cocking.

Employees or people here on company business, repeated the constable.

Mary was staring at Oscar. Her face was a desperate plea for him to say yes.

I am here on company business, said Oscar finally.

He can come with me den can't he? she said.

The guard rolled the pencil between his fingertips and chewed his lip.

It wouldn't be too much for me ta take her ta de ships down dere, Oscar added, with a patronising politeness that the constable regarded as typical of his class.

What do ye think? said the guard.

The constable flicked through the deck of cards, and nodded in cautious agreement.

Go on den, said the guard, and ye bring her back here in ten minutes.

Mary didn't hear the guard's last words, she was already through the pillars of the gates and ran to the first of four vessels that were tied to the quay and was asking the crew about Thomas' whereabouts

Oscar made no attempt to follow. He didn't want to interfere. He strolled down the narrow strip of quay between the brick buildings and the river with his hands tucked into his pockets as if he was having a leisurely walk along an English seaside promenade. It was a deliberate and arrogant gesture to signify his detachment from what was going on around him. But his intended audience, the workers, were too busy to grace him with any attention. Horse drawn bogies were hurrying up and down. Two derricks were hoisting bales of cotton from the second ship and the third ship was off-loading a dark powder into a metal bucket on a crane and then onto a small locomotive. Oscar peered into the hold. Inside was a gang of boys shovelling the clay furiously. They were completely covered in the fine black earth and the whites of their eyes shone out like the eyes of black men.

When he looked up Mary had vanished. Both hands flew out of his pockets. His fragile composure was shattered. His ward was lost and he would have to return to the gate alone to suffer a severe telling-off from the ill-tempered police constable. Then he caught a glimpse of her behind one of the bogies. She was light on her feet and when the wagon had passed hc saw her skipping into one of the buildings. Oscar crossed the rail tracks. He could see her through a doorway. She was talking to a tall young man with thick black hair that was bursting out from beneath his cap. She was pulling his arm to coax him outside. The young man resisted. He had other more pressing business to attend to and was directing her to wait outside.

Oscar sidled along to the next building. Through the filthy glass he could make out a large metal trough containing bubbling acid. Just above the surface was a steamy mist and it reminded him of a simmering cauldron. A man stood over the trough and was stirring the deadly liquid very gently with a long paddle. On his head he wore a rubber hat with the brim turned up. Hanging from his neck was a rubber apron that went all the way to his feet. He wore rubber boots and gloves that went up past his elbows. He had thick goggles and around his nose and mouth was a makeshift mask made of cloth.

The man hardly looked human. To Oscar he appeared terrifying and hideous. It was like some nightmare or what you might read about in a fantastic storybook. Above the trough was a ventilation shaft designed to take away the fumes. Oscar stared at this metal cone. It was corroded and rotting. The metal supporting the roof was rotting. The troughs and pipes were rotting and the man working there was rotting too. Eventually the acid would eat away at his lungs and make him ill and he would be dead long before his time had come.

Oscar remained by the window watching Mary from the corner of his eye. If she was aware of his presence she showed no sign of it. She was occupied entirely with the young man. And who was this Thomas? he wondered. Her boyfriend he supposed. That would explain her agitated state. Still, it surprised him. It was quite a contrast to the cool creature he had encountered in the doctor's house. Love did that to women. And then he thought, it had little to do with her sex.

The young man emerged after a short while and he guided Mary to the quay wall. The ship's moorings were being untied. The vessel was about to push off. What Oscar was witnessing however was no fond farewell. It was a final and permanent goodbye. The young man was gently spurning her, disentangling himself from the vines that had grown lovingly and tenderly around his body and his heart. She was in a haze and trembling. Was there anything more pathetic in the whole world than a clinging and needy lover being cast off, and still waiting for a crumb of affection to be thrown indifferently from the table? She was probably too young to understand that she would find another. There was always another. Love, for all of its lofty ideals, was ultimately a practical thing.

Finally the poor girl came to the point of resignation. There would be no cajoling. All her methods and wiles had been exhausted. They had worked in the past, not any more. The young man had made his mind up and there would be no reversal or capitulation. His heart had turned cold towards her. She went to take his hand. He gave it briefly then took it away. Someone on the ship was calling for him to get aboard. The ropes were all undone and the engines churned.

Come on lad, shouted the skipper from the wheelhouse.

The ship began edging away from the quay.

Thomas leapt down onto the deck, landing squarely on his feet and the vessel continued its progress towards the mouth of the river, leaving Mary alone on the quayside.

Oscar watched as Mary was engulfed by the workmen and women coming down the quay. They had arrived on a late train from Wexford and were walking briskly to make up for lost time. The constable came out of the hut, greeted them with his surly smile and was shouting at them to form a line. The colossal guard followed. He was accompanied by a young man with a pink complexion and blond thinning hair. He was in plus-fours and his shirt sleeves were rolled up securely as if he was ready to perform some serious work. The guard directed the man to Oscar.

One of Cocking's young acolytes, thought Oscar. There would be no evading him now.

The young man strided over purposefully and introduced himself.

I hear you might be joining us, said the young man.

He spoke like an English gentleman.

Not if I can help it, replied Oscar, and he replaced the cigarette he was about to light into the packet.

The young man was unsure if he was being sarcastic, and Oscar was pleased to have wrong-footed him.

Mister Cocking was tied up for a while, he said, to disguise his confusion.

Oh, I'm sure he's a busy chap, said Oscar, and he indicated for the young man to show the way.

They twisted and turned through a network of passages that ran between the warehouses and came out at four storey building with a steep wooden staircase on the outside.

Mister Cocking's on the top floor, said the young man, grabbing the handrail.

In the blink of an eye he was at the top with Oscar trailing behind. Once he'd mounted the last set of steps Oscar was given a moment to recover his breath and they stepped inside and walked along a dark corridor with creaking timbers. There were shoebox-sized offices on the left and right occupied by men in starched collars scribbling away like diligent administrators.

At the very end was an open door. Cocking was inside, seated behind a substantial oak desk.

He waved the young man away politely and directed Oscar to the couch while he continued sorting through a mass of unopened letters. Oscar sat cross-legged and took in his surroundings. It was all polished leather and wood and brass, just what he expected for the second in command of such an enterprise. And yet it was surprisingly compact, a bit like Cocking himself, nothing wasted, everything dedicated to the task at hand. The bookcase held thick volumes on engineering and chemistry, and on the wall in front of Oscar was a poster advertisement showing off the different size bullets and artillery shells made by Kynochs. They were all arranged in a pretty circle and the poster was lovingly framed like the print of a favourite painting or a family photograph.

It was dark in the office and Cocking was having difficulty reading.

Let's let some light in, shall we? he said, and he drew up the Venetian blinds.

Oscar got up off the couch to admire the expanse of sky and water to the east.

Magnificent sight isn't it, said Cocking, as he read some dull correspondence.

Oscar was about to begin eulogising the view. But Cocking wasn't referring to the scenery, he was referring to the factory. He caught himself before the mistake was made.

In that brief moment, before Oscar realised, he thought he had found some point in common with Cocking beyond the material world of the factory. If only Cocking had shown some kind of heart or soul. It would have made the whole sorry situation so much easier if he, just like Oscar, was actually trapped in this horrible circumstance. This, however, was precisely what Cocking was not. He was, down to his very core, a company man, an engineer, a maker of explosives. There was talk of little else at the meal in Oscar's house. The conversation was all about the marvels of cordite, and Oscar's father being an arch flatterer had indulged Cocking to the limit of everyone else's patience.

Cynical as he was, Oscar couldn't help being affected by the sight of the factory. The view revealed much more of it than could be seen from the road. The factory was vast, stretching right up to the next headland. He was unable to take it all in.

Yer little empire, he said.

Not so little, said Cocking, and he made a ball of the letter he was reading and tossed it into the bin. If it isn't the biggest factory in Ireland it's pretty damn close. The best part of five thousand people work here twenty-four hours a day. There's an endless demand for our products by the army and the navy, we can't make enough of it.

Oscar noted Cocking's self-confidence and satisfaction. It was not without good reason. It was Cocking who had convinced Chamberlain to take up the manufacture of this amazing new explosive called cordite, and it was Cocking who had suggested the town of Arklow as a good location with facilities to make the raw material needed, and a ready supply of cheap labour.

De war is good for business, said Oscar.

It's in the national interest that we make munitions, said Cocking.

De national interest is good for business den, said Oscar.

If you want to put it that way, said Cocking, then yes, and he ripped open a fresh envelope with a silver dagger.

If I had de choice it wouldn't be made at all, said Oscar.

A necessary evil I'm afraid.

Perhaps.

You must be glad you're Irish, said Cocking, no conscription for you lot.

Technically I'm Irish, said Oscar, and if dat's good enough to evade de army dat will do fine.

You're not a nationalist then? said Cocking, we don't want our explosives getting into the wrong hands.

And I taut all dose soldiers were here ta protect us against de Germans, said Oscar.

Cocking raised an eyebrow.

Both, he said, and he asked Oscar again if he was a nationalist.

De Irish call me English and de English call me Irish, said Oscar, but I have no loyalty ta anyone or anything.

Except pleasure, said Cocking.

Very perceptive, said Oscar.

Not really, said Cocking, you said so the other night.

Did I? said Oscar.

Cocking suddenly seemed uninterested. He'd finally found a letter of some importance. When he'd finished reading the communication he exhaled heavily. That's enough bureaucracy for one day, he said, and he threw the remaining unopened letters into a fancy mesh tray, and he went to the window.

Well, this is it, he said, and he made a grand sweeping gesture.

Below them was a large open square where all the activity of the factory converged. Cocking was jittery with pleasure at the sight. It was more like a train station than a factory. One track cut diagonally across the square. Running straight down the west side was another. A third track snuck down the side of a long, low building on the eastern edge and disappeared behind a peculiarly shaped wooden structure and out to the quay. Coming along this set of tracks was the locomotive Oscar had seen earlier, its solitary wagon loaded with the black earth from the ship on the quayside. Jets of steam hissed out from below the driver's cabin as it shunted along with sweaty determination, heading for one of the sheds.

Pyrites from Spain, explained Cocking, we roast them to extract ammonia gas.

Immediately north of the square was row upon row of tall cylindrical tanks and horizontal and vertical pipes.

And that, continued Cocking, is where the nitric and sulphuric acid for the cordite are made.

Fumes and vapours were leaking out everywhere.

It must be very dangerous, said Oscar.

We employ a lot of men, said Cocking, to read the thermometers, check the gauges, adjust valves, monitor levels to keep the beast at bay.

Then Cocking turned to the window overlooking the river.

And this is what it's all about, he said, and he pointed at the crates full of explosives on the bogie by the first steamer.

The magical cordite.

The magical cordite indeed, said Cocking, all on it's way to the arsenal at Woolwich.

You wouldn't realise it, he went on, but we're actually standing on an island, and he stamped his foot.

Oscar had been told the story many times of how an English engineer come to Arklow had outsmarted the local Irish lords.

This part of the factory was constructed twenty-five years ago as a chemical works, said Cocking, warming to his subject. The engineer came over from Newcastle and Lord Carlisle refused to sell him the plot of ground he wanted so the clever chap built an island on the floodplain between high and low tide.

Cocking's delight quickly waned.

About this job, he said, finally coming to the point, it's not an honorary position, you'll be trained, and there's a career in it if you're willing to work.

And what will ye have me do?

We'll put you in the shipping department first, said Cocking, see how you get on.

Oscar's gaze fell heavily to the floor.

You're under no obligation, said Cocking.

Oh I am, said Oscar, it's dis or the streets for me.

You think it's beneath you?

Oh, look I've no skill or profession, said Oscar, so I can hardly tink dat, still I don't relish de taut.

Try it for a little while, said Cocking, see how you get on and if you hate it...

Yes, said Oscar.

Anyway, the war is nearly over, added Cocking, a few months, a year at the most.

And de factory? asked Oscar, what happens to de town and de people?

I suspect we will be bought out by Imperial Chemicals, said Cocking, they want to monopolise the market and they will probably close this factory. We have interests in South Africa, mostly mining, we won't be going hungry.

And de town and all de people who work here?

Industries come and go, said Cocking, they always have and they always will.

And when you go?

To put it in layman's terms, said Cocking in a whisper, the town of Arklow is fucked.

CHAPTER 11

When Michael woke he was frightened and confused. The walls of his tiny bedroom were gone and he was lost in what seemed like an enormous open space. He sat bolt upright and gazed into the grey unfamiliar emptiness. And then he remembered. He was in one of the wards of the factory hospital. The terrible fear subsided and he lay down. His body still ached from the beating he'd received. It was particularly sore when he took a breath. He dismissed the pain. There was no serious damage, the nurse from Dublin had said so, just a lot of bruising. It was nothing compared to the condition of the men around him.

He slid out from under the covers, pulled up the sagging pyjamas the nurse had given him, and he tiptoed over to Seanee and sat down on a stool beside his bed.

His friend's torso and upper arms were covered in bandages and they had a strong smell of some ointment.

Are ye asleep? asked Michael, and he nudged Seanee's leg roughly.

Asleep, repeated Seanee, without opening his eyes, I've hardly slept since de explosion.

The words came out with great difficulty as if they had travelled from some dark, hollow region very far inside him.

Can I have a drink of whaa-ter? he asked, I can't ever get enough whaa-ter inta me.

Michael picked up a white enamel cup from the bedside table. Attached to the cup was a rubber tube and Michael directed it into his friend's mouth. Seanee's tongue came out and he bit onto the tube with his two remaining teeth.

He sucked the cup dry in one long, lazy draught.

Aaahh, he said with a smack of his lips, and Michael put the cup down.

I bet it's not as good as a pint, said Michael, and Seanee rocked slightly in agreement.

The dawn was creeping in through a break in the curtains and Michael could see the raw wounds on his friend's face.

Pretty ain't it, that's what Seanee said every time he saw Michael looking at his scorched flesh.

Dat's notin, he went on, ye should see de rest a me, I look like a giant fried rasher.

It should've been me, said Michael.

But it wasn't was it, said Seanee, so stop frettin yerself about it.

I can't help it, said Michael.

Jaysus man, said Seanee, and he twisted his body to look at Michael, you'd prefer ta be lyin here instead a me, would ye?

No, said Michael.

Well den, said Seanee, and he rolled back to his original position.

Apart from some slight jerking movements in his right arm he was practically motionless. It was not a tranquil state. When he did move, he wriggled. He was trying to worm his way out of the oily bandages. Michael was amazed that his friend didn't complain more about the extreme pain and discomfort he had to endure.

Does it hurt? asked Michael.

I don't tink dere's anytin dere ta hurt, said Seanee, most of my skin is gone. Anyway, I'm full a morphine. I'm hallucinatin half de time, I can see rats and spiders crawlin up me bed.

It's better dan the pain I suppose, said Michael.

Seanee wiggled his fingers. He wanted more water.

Michael filled the cup from a jug on the table and he stuck the tube in Seanee's mouth again. He drank very slowly this time. He was having difficulty holding the tube with his two rotting teeth and water was dribbling down his chin.

Michael dabbed the charred skin beneath his lower lip with the sleeve of his pyjamas and Seanee shook his head angrily so Michael pulled his sleeve away.

Don't do dat, said Seanee, and he heaved in a rasping breath and let it out.

Sorry, said Michael.

How are you doin anyway? asked Seanee.

I'm still alive, said Michael.

Not so pretty now are ye without that tooth? said Seanee.

Michael's tongue danced around the spot where his right front tooth used to be.

If it wasn't for dem soldiers, said Michael, I tink dose bastards from Wexford would've beaten me ta death.

Had dis dispute anytin ta do with dat woman?

No, snorted Michael, and I won't be goin near her any time soon.

Dat would be a very wise decision, said Seanee.

Do ye remember anytin about the explosion?

No, said Seanee, it wasn't me dat caused it though, dat's for sure, I didn't even get me foot inside de hut and I was blasted out. What difference does it make anyway? I'm well and truly fucked.

A serious-looking young nurse was at the entrance to the ward with a trolley full of medicine and bandages. They would be drawing the curtains soon. Michael said goodbye to his friend and he went back to his bed and he fell into a heavy sleep.

When he woke again it was mid-morning and most of the patients on the ward had long risen. Some lay flat in their beds, too ill to sit up. Those in better condition were reading papers or talking with their neighbours or walking about.

The sun was climbing up above the eastern horizon. Michael thought the ward had a kind of heavenly radiance. The windows looked out over the sea and the light shimmered against the brilliant white walls and the polished floor. The uniform rows of beds, the big clock measuring out time, and the pungent odour of iodine reminded Michael of the calm and order of a convent or a monastery. He ran his rough hands over the crisp white linen and the new feather pillow and an inner peace descended upon him. It was, as always, short-lived. It was taken over by another considerable less pleasant sensation, his realization of the suffering around him. Many of the men were coughing and vomiting. In the bed opposite was a chap of about his own age who had acid spilt on his left hand and his face. He was in a kind of shock and uttered not one word. Beside him was a boy who'd lost three fingers while playing with guncotton he'd smuggled out of the factory.

At noon a man of about twenty-eight years dressed in a neat army uniform came into the ward with the nurse from Dublin.

They went directly to Seanee's bed.

Sean, Sean!

The nurse was talking into his ear.

Dere's a doctor here to see you, she said.

A tiny shudder went through his body.

I was nearly dreaming, he said, and he raised his right hand a fraction.

The doctor took it with extraordinary firmness and said his name was Peter.

Are ye gonna fix me up? asked Seanee.

I've just come for a peek really, said Peter.

Where's de other fella? asked Seanee, Keogh or whatever his fecken name is.

101

He'll be back tomorrow, said the nurse.

Dat's a pity, said Seanee, he's a fecken arsehole.

Peter was holding back a laugh as he cut part of the bandage below Seanee's shoulder. He examined the damaged skin beneath very closely.

How come yer wearin dat uniform if yer a doctor? asked Seanee.

I'm a doctor in de army, said Peter.

So what are ye doin here den? asked Seanee.

Is dat any of your bloody business? said the nurse.

I'm just confabulatin, said Seanee.

I've been asked ta help out a little, said Peter.

I suppose dis isn't very stimulatin? continued Seanee.

Stimulating? said Peter. He was puzzled by the questions.

After what yev seen in France, said Seanee, you were in France weren't ye? I can see it in yer eyes.

The front is certainly...interesting, said Peter.

I'd say yev seen a ting or two?

We've got a lot of full thickness burns here, said the nurse, deliberately interrupting Seanee.

From acid spills? asked Peter.

Yes, said the nurse.

And de odd explosion, added Seanee.

Yes, I heard about dat, said Peter, and he replaced the bandage over Seanee's chest.

What are ye using on dere? he asked the nurse, and she went to a medicine cupboard and came back with a large silver tin.

Peter inspected the label and then he twisted the top off and sniffed the yellow cream inside.

And we use bicarbonate of soda on the acid burns, said the nurse.

You should try Number 7 paraffin, said Peter, we've used it in France and found it much better dan dese wax-based ointments.

How do you apply it? asked the nurse.

With a camelhair brush, said Peter, and ye should dress de wound with cotton rather than wool.

She's a nice lookin girl, isn't she? said Seanee.

Oh for goodness sake! said the nurse, go-awn back ta yer silly dreams.

Don't ye want to hear what it was about? said Seanee.

No I bloody well don't, said the nurse.

Right so, said Seanee.

A man on the other side of the ward was vomiting into a metal bowl. He retched repeatedly. It was his second bout of throwing up and all he had managed to produce for his strenuous efforts was a dribble of sticky bile.

How long has he been ill? asked Peter.

He was admitted early dis mornin, said the nurse.

Nitrous fumes?

Yes, said the nurse, a lot of de men here are brought in sufferin from de effect of fumes, or acid burns. De coughin helps clear the congestion.

Peter sidestepped the nurse into the centre of the ward.

How does it progress? he asked.

He was speaking in a near whisper.

Dere's no need ta lower your voice, said the nurse, dese men understand very well what's goin on.

Peter nodded and apologised.

Dere are some fatalities, said the nurse, others recover quite well, the rest, especially de older ones, will never work again.

Aren't dere any signs warnin de men?

Everywhere, said the nurse, and masks are provided for dose in de most frequent contact. But de fumes are hard to contain and dere's no odour so dose without just have ta be vigilant.

Have ye had many cases?

Over eight hundred patients since de hospital opened, said the nurse, about a third are acid poisonin.

Peter let out a small whistle.

Yes, she said, it's quite a lot.

How can dere be so many?

The factory is working flat out, said the nurse, safety is not a priority.

And de treatment?

For nitrous fumes, dere's none really, said the nurse, except oxygen.

Peter loosened his tie.

And dis young man here? he asked

He was at the foot of Michael's bed.

Oh, ye don't need to worry about dat one, said the nurse, he's been carousin.

If ye mean I was inebriated and got inta a fight, said Michael, well dat's not the case.

I was only jokin, said the nurse, and she patted his leg.

I was attacked outside a pub, said Michael.

He got a knock on de head, added the nurse, some bruisin to his ribs and a broken tooth.

Did ye lose consciousness at all? asked Peter.

Nope, replied Michael.

Yer de fittest man in here, said the nurse.

Have you had any dizziness?

No, said Michael.

Peter was about to move on but he returned to Michael's bed.

Yer hands, he said.

104

What about dem? said Michael, and he brought them up to his chest.

Dat eczema is quite bad, said Peter.

Go easy, said the nurse to Michael, he's not goin ta eat ye.

Michael relaxed himself a little and returned his hands to his side.

Peter bent over to examine the dried skin.

Do ye see dis often? Peter asked the nurse.

Occasionally with de men in the engineerin works, said the nurse, it's caused by de lubricants.

Do you work in de engineering works? asked Peter.

No, said Michael, I'm operatin a cordite press most of de time.

And ye handle cordite paste?

Hapes of it, said Michael.

With yer bare hands?

I don't know of any other way ta fill a press, said Michael.

Why don't ye wear gloves? asked Peter.

Most of de men refuse ta wear gloves, said the nurse, they can't grip anytin properly.

Um, said Peter, well de eczema is probably a reaction ta de mercury, I was readin about it last night in de safety manual.

Dere's only tiny amounts in de paste? insisted the nurse.

Well dere's one way ta tell for certain, said Peter, and he asked Michael if he could look at his gums.

Naw, said Michael, yer alright.

Michael, just do as the doctor asks, said the nurse.

I'd be careful if I was you, chipped in Seanee from across the ward, dat chap bites.

Dis doctor doesn't work here Michael, said the nurse, he can't stop ye from workin.

Michael sat forward a fraction and Peter raised his top lip.

Ye see, said Peter, and he indicated with his little finger to a faint blue line above Michael's teeth.

The nurse squinted and then blinked in affirmation.

Do ye get headaches? asked Peter.

Michael refused to answer.

I'm only concerned about yer health, said Peter.

Michael gazed at him blankly.

Ye may be sufferin from poisonin, said Peter.

Let me do de frettin about me health not you, said Michael.

But Peter pressed him further.

Have ye lost yer appetite? Are ye nervous or anxious, overly-irritated or depressed?

Still Michael refused to answer.

At least tell me if ye wash yer hands regularly? asked Peter.

I'm not a fecken knacker, said Michael.

Don't talk ta de man like dat, said Seanee.

Yeah, said Michael, I wash me hands as often as I can.

Good, said Peter, and try ta avoid wipin them in yer work clothes.

Can I go now? said Michael, and he asked for his clothes.

His friend Jimmy was at the door of the ward beckoning to him.

Michael and Jimmy found a table in the backroom of The Harbour Bar. All along the counter thirsty customers were waiting impatiently for service. The clock was moving dangerously close to two. There would be no drink after that, the police constables and the soldiers were coming back and they would see to that.

So what's the big news?

First tings first now, said Jimmy, what are ye havin?

I don't want anytin, said Michael.

Just de one, said Jimmy, ta celebrate.

Ta celebrate what?

Jimmy clapped his hands together loudly.

Dere's jobs goin up at de nitro houses and you and me have got a start up dere next week.

I don't want ta work up dere, said Michael.

The words were said so softly they were inaudible.

So what's yer poison?

What's yer poison? What's yer poison. Michael heard the question echoing over and over inside his head.

Well?

Jimmy was clicking his fingers together.

I told ye I don't want one.

So what did ye come here for den? asked Jimmy.

Because ye asked me ta.

Ah, what de devil is wrong with ye?

I feel queer.

Well, yer certainly actin queer.

Go on den, said Michael, two bottles.

Good man, said Jimmy, and off he went to get served.

An elderly man and his wife were stationed behind the bar and they presented an almost comic contrast to the great urgency of their customers. They moved with absolutely no sense of rush. They worked at the same rate as if the place was empty, carrying their ancient bodies up and down the same twelve foot stretch they'd been carrying them up and down for forty odd years. And they had no reason to rush. They'd made more money in the past three years than they had in the twenty before and it mattered little to them if they sold one more pint or ten more. The men hated them for their indifference - what could they do, only continue with their desperate pleas to be served by rattling their coins.

After a good ten minutes Jimmy returned with the drinks.

Yer probably outta sorts after seein Seanee, he said.

Dat doctor reckons I'm bein poisoned by mercury.

Puuhhh! said Jimmy, and he poured his drink skilfully into a pint glass. He watched and waited impatiently for it to settle and he knocked back a fair portion of it.

Dere's fuck all mercury in dat paste, he said, and he replaced the glass on the table with a great sigh of satisfaction.

Michael rubbed his hands. They were oily from the cream the nurse had put on them.

Well, don't get over excited, said Jimmy.

About what?

About yer new job!

I don't want ta work in dere.

It's de best paid work in de whole factory.

Dat's because it's de most dangerous work in de whole factory.

For twenty shillins a week I'll take me chances, said Jimmy.

Most men wouldn't do it, not for any money, said Michael.

I'm not like most men.

No, a course not, said Michael, yer like a god or sometin. I'm just flesh and blood, the same as Seanee.

Ah! Poor auld Seanee, said Jimmy, how is he?

Ye could've found out yerself...if yed bothered ta talk ta him.

I don't like hospitals.

Nobody likes hospitals.

Anyway, said Jimmy, what about dis job?

You make me fuckin laugh Jimmy, said Michael, dere ye were rarin up on me about how dangerous it was workin with cordite paste now we're gonna be workin with nitro.

Yeah well...tings have changed, said Jimmy.

What's changed? asked Michael, even though he had a good idea what the answer was.

I don't want ta go into it.

In dat case you do what ye like, said Michael, I'm not stoppin ye workin dere.

I don't wanna go up dere on me own.

You don't want dis, you don't dat, said Michael, but ye want me ta go up dere with ye.

Look, one a de jobs is mixin nitro and guncotton, said Jimmy, any eejit could do it.

I don't want ta work dere, repeated Michael.

Jaysus look at de time, said Jimmy, and he shot up from his seat, de missus'll go mad.

He finished the remainder of his stout.

Just try it for a couple a weeks, said Jimmy, ye'll have a few bob more.

I'll tink about it, said Michael.

Have a tink about it, he said, and if you don't like it, ye can go back ta de press house.

I said I'll tink about it.

Ye won't let me down will ye?

We'll see.

Good man, said Jimmy, we'll go over there later on this afternoon, and he left.

CHAPTER 12

Oscar was sitting with a mug of stewed tea. He was watching a table full of chattering women. There was one, a tall girl, who he found very pretty. Her drab factory clothes and hat couldn't conceal the beauty that lay beneath. And the girl was more than happy to return his attentions. The other girls told her to stop and she said she would do as she pleased. She wasn't the first to have caught his eye. The factory was full of pretty things easily flattered by a second glance or an admiring look. He would have to restrain himself and not let his vanity get the better of him. Cocking had warned him against getting involved with female workers. It would be bad for the company, Cocking said, and you might get more than you bargained for. Oscar was beginning to understand what he meant. In a corner of the canteen was a man in his early twenties with another much older man. They were engaged in a heated discussion and the arrival of the women seemed to aggravate the young man. His face was bruised, his front tooth was broken and his knuckles were swollen. Not someone to be trifled with, thought Oscar. And the girl's flirtation with Oscar was upsetting the young man intensely. She was obviously trying to provoke him and her scheme was working very well indeed. The young man was losing control of his temper. It was like the devil had got inside him. Luckily for Oscar he was in two minds as to where to direct his anger and the older man seized upon his indecision to cool the young man down. A few more strong words passed between them and after some cajoling the old man persuaded the younger one to leave.

There were still a few sparks left in him though. He veered towards Oscar intent upon an argument but the old man pushed his friend the other way, and out the door the two of them went, still snapping and snarling at each other.

Once they were gone Oscar forgot the two men and the pretty girl. He sipped his tea and fretted over a pile of papers waiting on his desk. He could hardly bring himself to return. All day long the clerks talked about this form and that ledger. The entire business was a mystery to him. And there was never a spare minute for anyone to explain. It was precisely as he had predicted. He was useless. Comments had already been made by the office manager about his tardiness and general lack of interest. He would have happily changed places with one of the factory labourers. He watched them from his window. They at least were allowed some freedom and weren't confined to a desk. And their physical work seemed more noble and honest to him than the affairs of the bookkeepers and clerks who calculated the profits of the worker's efforts. Oscar had said as much to his co-workers, partly to shock them, but he meant what he said, and they regarded him strangely and passed him off as a hypocrite hired because of his family connections.

Oscar finished his tea and as he left the canteen he was greeted by another clerk from his office.

Might you do me a favour? said Oscar.

Well dat depends what it is, replied the clerk, sensing some mischief.

Will ye tell dat manager of ours dat I'm feeling unwell?

Why don't ye go an tell him yerself?

I'd prefer not to.

And what exactly is it dat's ailin ye? Just in case I'm asked, said the clerk, a headache, a belly ache, or a hangover perhaps?

Humm! A headache will probably be best, said Oscar.

He won't like it, said the clerk, he won't like it one little bit, yer already in de fecken doghouse with him.

Well I'll be in de double doghouse den, said Oscar, and he thanked the man and left.

He went out of the factory gates, up the quay and he walked slowly towards his house. He felt incredible relief. Of course it was only a respite. Cocking would be informed of his ineptitude and general lack of interest. He would get a telling off on his return. Then his father would be told. He could already hear the lecture. Oscar would take it like he took all the other lectures and rantings, letting it wash over him, ignoring the obvious hypocrisy

He approached his house tentatively. The motor car was nowhere to be seen. His father had gone out as he said he intended to do. Perhaps he had taken his mother along. That would be a mercy, to be spared her questions and concerns. The front door creaked as he entered and the housekeeper's head appeared at the kitchen door.

Ye can come in, she said, de master has gone out for de day with yer good mother.

Oscar relaxed.

Yer cousin's about somewhere, she added, and she disappeared.

He spied into the sitting room and saw the lonely and silent piano. He crept inside, sat down at the polished instrument, lifted the lid and searched out an old familiar song. After a few attempts he got it half right. It was one of those tunes full of memories that made him sad.

Then his playing ceased. There was a face at the door. It was his cousin.

What on earth are ye doin here? asked Peter.

Come in, come in, said Oscar, and he got up, pulled his cousin inside and closed the door.

Do ye remember dis one? asked Oscar, and his hands moved clumsily over the keys.

Peter grimaced and covered his ears.

Oh come on Peter, said Oscar, and he hummed the melody that his fingers had failed to produce.

She's My Little Sweetheart, said Peter.

Oscar snapped his fingers.

Dat's de one, he said, and he started to decipher another song.

Shouldn't you be workin?

What? said Oscar. He was busy following a sequence of chords.

Shouldn't you be workin?

I was feelin a bit sick, said Oscar, and he played a verse of the song and sang the few bits of the lyrics that were still in his head.

Sick indeed, said Peter.

It was a good life we had back den, he said, we knew how ta enjoy ourselves.

We did little else, said Peter.

And now I'm stuck in dat damn factory.

Ye make it sound like a predicament, said Peter, a more reasonable man would have been relieved. Ye could be doin sometin considerably less agreeable and yet ye just sulk and pine for de self-indulgent life ye had in London.

I'm not a reasonable man, said Oscar, I never have been, dat's one of de reasons you like me.

Liked, said Oscar, past tense?

It's hard ta hate someone who makes ye laugh.

You haven't made me laugh in a long time.

Oscar played a ridiculous comedy song and threw himself off the stool like a clown.

Yer laughin now, he said.

Only because yer so utterly pathetic, said Peter.

What's it like? asked Oscar.

113

What's what like?

De front?

Oh, it's too gloomy ta talk about.

Tell me about it, said Oscar.

Why?

Because I want ta know, said Oscar.

Peter rubbed his tired eyes with his knuckles, lit a cigarette and picked a shred of loose tobacco off his tongue.

I was in such a mad rush ta get myself inta dat damn war, said Peter. I taut I'd seen it all in dat Red Cross hospital in London and when I arrived at de base hospital in Trouville I managed alright. A lot of de men were sufferin from de usual diseases of civil life, most of em should never have been allowed ta enlist in de first fecken place. A few days in de trenches and dey were knocked right out. I had so much free time dere I went out on a few expeditions ta collect butterflies and flowers, can ye believe dat? But I didn't realise I had it so good and I pushed one of de surgeons ta get me moved up ta a casualty clearin station, right up in the thick of it.

Be careful what ye wish for boy, said Oscar.

Indeed, said Peter, my wish came true after two weeks and I was off ta Crouay. I had a couple a days ta settle in and I quickly realized I was way outta me depth. All de other doctors were much younger dan me and had a year or two of experience. On my first day I was given de job of reception officer and I was left with two orderlies and one other doctor in dis dimly lit tent. Dat doctor was Catherine's husband. Anyway, for two days thousands of men and pieces of equipment had been movin up de road to Amiens ta support an attack on Villers-Bretonneux. Jaysus, I've never seen anytin like it, nor likely to again. De massacre began dat evenin and at two in de mornin de ambulances came rollin in. Dey came in such numbers, on stretchers or stumblin, all in khaki, wrapped in blankets and

114

coats, bandaged and splintered, stiff with mud and blood and dust and sweat and salt and shite, with labels attached describin their injuries, can ye believe dat, labels like de price tags in expensive shops. I hadn't a clue what ta do with all dese men, I had no instructions, no trainin. Catherine's husband helped me though, whisperin suggestions as we went. We had de stretcher cases on one side and de standin cases on de other. Den I worked me way through de ones for resuss, preop or de evacuation tent. And de most incredible ting of all was dat, in dis place of pain and misery dere was silence, no moans, no groans, not a word of complaint. De badly shocked had passed beyond it. The rest were numb or too tired ta speak, or so exhausted dey slept standin up. Dese poor men, God help dem, had shattered heads, disfigured faces, stumps for limbs. A lot of dem had shells or bullet wounds in de chest and were spitting blood and gaspin for breath. Worst of all were de ones with de innocent little mark where de bullet had entered hidin de hopeless disaster within. It was a terrible ting, havin ta choose dose who were ta be operated upon and dose dat were ta be left to die. And de irony was we picked dose dat we could make fit enough to send back ta de front.

Peter lit another cigarette.

It was seven in de mornin before de entire tent was cleared, tree hours later I had ta begin operatin on de same men. I got a wash, some breakfast and at ten I was back operatin. I was so tired and I hadn't de slightest idea how to deal with de terrible wounds. My assistant could see it plainly, and I taut what bad luck it was for de wretched victims who came under my knife. First to be savaged by de enemy and den by me. Dey went under de ether happily, dependin on my skill ta mend dere bodies and save dere lives, it would've been far better for dem if fate had sent dem ta de next table. At one point I went to take a cigarette break and I wandered inta an outbuildin away from de pandemonium. It was filled with corpses. So I went inta de next buildin along and dere I found a heap of freshly amputated arms and legs perhaps ten feet high.

Ye see, said Peter, my hands are shakin just rememberin it. Anyway, when I came out I bumped into Catherine's husband. I was on the verge of cryin. I can't remember what it was he said, whatever it was it gave me de courage to carry on and I went back ta work. Dat dreadful dreadful day ended at seven in de evenin, after tirty-six hours of continuous work. I was exhausted with anxiety and fatigue and couldn't see how I could go through de same ordeal again. Givin up was even worse though and after a long sleep I woke to a glorious July day. We were camped on farmland untouched by de war. The air was alive with de sound of larks and de fields were decorated with poppies and marigolds. It was perfectly calm, if only I could forget de harrowin scenes inside de tents. Still, dere were only a few cases left from de night before and in de early afternoon I was able ta get out among de birds and butterflies and flowers. It was dat walk and Catherine's husband dat saved me, and got me through it. I got time alone ta pull meself together and so many times afterwards I had ta face de equal of dat night but I never became overwhelmed with de same panic of dat first experience.

Catherine's husband and I became very good friends after dat, said Peter, and now I feel I owe him sometin.

He left her here, said Oscar, he abandoned her, left her ta dat old witch of a mother-in-law.

It's justa fling for you isn't it?

For fuck's sake Peter, don't bloody well go on about it.

When I get back ta France I want ta assure him dat everytin is alright.

I don't like bein told what to do.

De war will be over soon, yer fader will die and den ye can go back ta London. A man could still live a very comfortable life on de money you'll inherit.

116

Yev clearly given it a lot of taut, said Oscar.

It doesn't take much taut, said Peter. Are dere any letters?

A few I wrote while I was in Paris.

False ardour no doubt.

It wasn't at de time.

And now?

I don't know, said Oscar, and pray tell, what do you do Peter ta satisfy your manly urges?

I don't have other men's wives, said Peter.

No, of course not, said Oscar, in dat department yer completely moral.

CHAPTER 13

The wind was blowing in through the holes and crevices around the door and the tiny windows. It was whining and cursing damnation against those inside. You're not welcome here, it was saying, this is not your domain. Some of the old fishermen swore there were demons in the river. Michael didn't believe a word of it. Nothing, not even a devil could reside in the shit and filth that flowed down from the mines and out from the factory. But inside Hut Number 189 in the dark of night, with the roaring sea a few dozen feet away, and its angry cousin banging on the walls, it was easy to believe in unearthly things that could do you harm.

Michael shifted his gaze away from the rattling window only to look back as another gust crashed against it.

Yer first shift? asked the other man, whose name was Kavanagh, and he directed Michael to a pile of sturdy wooden boxes in a corner.

Michael had to concentrate to decipher the man's muddy accent. After a few seconds he said yes and he took one of the empty boxes and placed it on the weighing scale.

Well never mind de noise, said the man, just cape yer mind on de business at hand, dis is no spot for dreamin.

Can I blow me nose? said Michael.

Blow away, said Kavanagh, and he bent down to check the weights dangling from the scales.

In front of the scales was a silver tank about four feet in diameter and seven feet in height. Fitted to the base of the tank was a flexible pipe that served as a tap. The pipe was held upright by a loop of string attached to the tank. Kavanagh removed the string, lowered the pipe and a clear liquid poured into the box. He moved the pipe in a circular motion and a thin foamy head appeared on the surface.

Kavanagh petted the tank with his free hand.

How much nitro would you estimate to be inside der now? he asked.

Michael had already conducted a quiet calculation on this very question.

A good six hundred gallons, he said.

Yer not far off, said Kavanagh, with a complimentary wink.

She's some piece a work I tell ye, he continued, and he knocked on the metal container with the knuckle of his middle finger, half an inch of steel dere.

Ye don't wanna do dat too hard, said Michael.

Kavanagh stroked the cool metal to reassure Michael.

And do ye know what we call dis beast? he said.

No, said Michael, trying to add hint of curiosity.

We call it *The Stallion*, said Kavanagh, and he leaned in over the box and stuck his crotch near the base of the pipe.

The girls ed love me if I had a lad dat big.

Who's dreamin now? asked Michael.

Ah sure, I wouldn't have a notion what ta do with it, admitted Kavanagh.

When the scales tipped up Kavanagh raised the pipe carefully, secured it back in the upright position and he spat on his hands.

Ye git a bitter grip widda bit of spit boy, said Kavanagh, and Michael followed his example and spat on both his palms.

Right, said Kavanagh, on the count of tree, one---two---tree, and together they carried the box over to a narrow table in the centre of the hut.

Easy boy, easy, said Kavanagh.

119

Michael jerked the box and Kavanagh had to drop his end quickly to prevent the nitro from splashing.

What in de name a God is wrong with ye? demanded Kavanagh.

Michael shook a bit and wiped a band of icy perspiration from his upper lip.

Jaysus boy, be careful or ye'll kill us both, said Kavanagh, and he clicked his fingers and told Michael to bring him the guncotton.

Michael grabbed a bulging cloth sack from a pile by the door and he passed it to Kavanagh.

The top was gathered together by a knot tied like a shoelace. Kavanagh yanked hard at the knot and the top of the sack fell open.

Michael took a handful of the cotton and let it fall into the nitroglycerine.

Looks as harmless as snowflakes.

Harmless me arse, said Kavanagh, and he told Michael to stand back a bit.

Some lads react quite bad to de dust off dis stuff, he explained.

Michael withdrew and Kavanagh upended the sack, took a step back from the box himself, and allowed the cotton to fall in a heap into the nitroglycerine.

Then he gave the sack a good shake that produced a cloud of fine cotton dust.

Ye can git stuck inta dat when yer ready, said Kavanagh.

Michael rolled up his shirt sleeves as far as they would go, waited until the dust had settled and began working cotton into the nitroglycerine.

Mix her up good boy, said Kavanagh.

Michael spied on his co-worker as he leaned against a narrow wooden pillar gnawing at the horrible remains of his fingernails.

120

He was well over fifty years of age, an old man in Michael's eyes. He was slight to the point of malnourishment. The stickman, as Michael was calling him in his head, had gigantic bushy, grey eyebrows. More grey hairs were sprouting like dry roots out of his nostrils and his ears. His pants were held up by a piece of twine that was frayed at both ends, and they were too big in the waist and too short in the leg.

Where are ye from? asked Michael.

Out west, said the man.

Out west where?

I owned a small bit of land and a few cattle in Galway, Kavanagh explained. Me wife died five years ago from some sort of tumour dat wasted her away ta notin. Once she was dead and buried in de ground me two daughters ran off ta America, never ta be heard of again. Den de news came to my remote part of de world dat dere was work ta be had in de town of Arklow so I left Galway and de farm. I was sick ta death of it anyway, sick of walkin around up ta me arse in muck and shite so I came ta work in de factory.

Michael listened as he kneaded the paste and after five minutes the cotton and nitroglycerine had formed into a dry, sticky mass that was hard to work. Michael was up to his elbows in the stuff and was panting from the effort.

Yer doin a fine job boy, said Kavanagh, ye wouldn't last long on a farm though, not at de rate yer goin.

Michael eased up a bit.

All de fecken machinery dey have in dis factory and we have to do dis with our bare hands.

It's a fierce delicate operation, said Kavanagh, requirin de human touch.

It's like mixin dough.

It even ends up in an oven, said Kavanagh, well ye'll be well aware a dat.

Michael's motion ceased.

What do ye mean?

Don't be gitten all uppety now, said Kavanagh.

I didn't so much as set foot inside de hut dat blew up, said Michael.

So I heard, said Kavanagh.

As long as we're clear on dat point, said Michael.

Crystal, said Kavanagh.

Good, said Michael, and he went back to his mixing.

Wexford men don't wanna work with ye all de same, added Kavanagh.

And I don't wanna ta work with dem, said Michael.

So what are ye doin all de way down here den? enquired Kavanagh, ye must be desperate for a dollar.

Not as desperate as ye might tink, said Michael, what's your excuse?

Kavanagh pondered this for some while.

Ah, I doe know, he said, with a violent scratch of his shiny scalp, makes no odds, I'm here now.

Very philosophical, said Michael.

Dey say yer bad luck, said Kavanagh.

I am, said Michael, without raising his head from the task.

No such ting as luck, good or bad, said Kavanagh, chewing on the tiny remains of his left thumbnail, not as far as I can make out anyways, only carelessness and stupidity.

So I'm stupid am I?

More careless I'd say, said Kavanagh, probably not your fault though.

What are ye sayin?

Kavanagh wriggled his hips and pulled up his sagging pants.

Cool yer boilers, he said, and he grabbed a lump of paste and squeezed it in his fist until it oozed out between his long fingers.

Dat should do it, he said, and the two men placed the box by the door and started the same process all over again.

Ye didn't answer me question, said Michael to Kavanagh as the man filled another empty box with nitroglycerine.

Ye take offense quare easy boy.

Yer givin me cause for offense.

I surely am not, said Kavanagh, I've never seen the like of it except me wife. She was like dat and I'm sure dat was de seed of de death dat ate her insides.

Michael sneezed. His nose was running. He threw his head back then forward and forced as much snot as he could into his old handkerchief. When he'd finished the yellow rag was wet through.

I'm puttin dis on here to dry if ye don't object? said Michael, and he opened out the cloth and laid it on the hot water pipe that fed into the only radiator in the hut.

Kavanagh cracked his knuckles.

Don't leave dat on dere, he said.

Why not? asked Michael indignantly.

Because dat pipe's hotter dan hell.

Dat's why I'm puttin it dere.

Kavanagh went over to the radiator, pinched the corner of the rag and removed it.

It'll go on fire, explained Kavanagh, and he glided a fingertip quickly across the pipe.

And what would ye say dis is? he continued.

Dust a course, said Michael.

Guncotton dust, said Kavanagh, de room's full of it, one tiny flame and dis hut goes to the moon. Didn't anyone tell ye in the last place.

No radiators in dere, said Michael, taking the handkerchief.

It was already drying out, another few minutes and it would've been scorched and ignited.

123

Run dat brush over dose pipes and de radiator, said Kavanagh.

Sitting on the narrow window ledge was a brush with fine bristles.

Go on, get down dere and clean it, said Kavanagh.

Michael got on his knees and did as the old farmer told him.

After he was done the two men, fed up with each other, refrained from further conversation.

They laboured on through the night repeating the routine of filling the boxes with nitroglycerine, adding the guncotton and kneading it into a paste. They spoke only when the task required it. The pace, set by Kavanagh, was slow and steady. The only break in the monotony was the arrival every hour or so of a little man in rubber boots and a raincoat who came to take away the filled boxes.

An hour before the end of the shift the nitroglycerine ran out.

Come on with me, said Kavanagh.

Why? asked Michael.

I need to git the foreman ta run a load down inta de tank, explained Kavanagh.

I'll wait here, said Michael.

Ye can't, said Kavanagh, taking off his apron, dere has ta be two men in here at all times, and he tossed Michael his coat.

Outside the wind had abated. They took a long gravel path up a steep bank. They were less than a third of the way up and Michael was out of breath.

We'll take a break, said Kavanagh.

I'm alright, said Michael.

He was bent over with his hands resting on his knees sucking in air.

You don't look alright, said Kavanagh.

I said I'm grand.

Go easy boy, said Kavanagh, ye'll git notin for killin yerself in dis job.

I've only come up dat path, said Michael, how could I be so fucked?

It's de nitro, said Kavanagh, affects de heart and de lungs, didn't yer friend Jimmy tell ye?

No, said Michael, it doesn't seem ta bother you.

It gits ta lads in different ways and at different times, said Kavanagh, I suffer from fierce bad headaches and sometimes I see tings dat aren't dere.

Like what?

Rats, big spiders, said Kavanagh, like morphine I'm told.

Dat's not nitro, said Michael, dat's drink.

I don't drink, said Kavanagh, never have, not a drop, took the oath when I was confirmed. Me auld fella used ta throw it into himself, couldn't git it down his greedy fecken throat fast enough. I didn't much like what it did to him either, made em quare mean.

It's been turnin my auld fella into a soppy eejit dese days, said Michael.

It'll do dat too, said Kavanagh.

Michael straightened himself up to resume the climb and Kavanagh pressed him gently on the shoulder forcing him down onto the grass by the side of the path.

Sit up, said Kavanagh, and Michael rested himself against a slender wooden pole that was supporting a sagging telephone wire.

It was still dark but light enough to distinguish the terrain below. Dotted around like carelessly tossed stones were dozens of little pitched roofs peaking up above the mounds of sand that encircled them. Bogies moved slowly along the tracks between the huts with lanterns leading the way. Some were drawn by horses, others were pushed by invisible men.

It's like a city, said Kavanagh.

City of death, said Michael.

City of death indeed, said Kavanagh.

I'd only saw de sea once before I came east, continued Kavanagh, now I come out here and dis wild, crazy ting is roarin at me every day.

It's a bit spooky here at night, said Michael.

I listen ta dem waves, said Kavanagh, and de odd time I'm convinced dere's men out dere screamin. It's all in me head a course. It's de fecken nitro, it's weird stuff boy.

Michael found a sea shell and he tossed it into a deep gully beside the path. A moment later there was a hollow clank.

What de hell's dat?

An empty drum, said Kavanagh, dey dump dem down in dat hole.

Michael hissed and raised himself up using the pole for support.

Let's go, he said, and he struggled up the path behind Kavanagh.

At the top was the road. To the right was the Spion Kop headland. To the left was the enormous mound surrounding the four buildings where the nitroglycerine was made.

Two soldiers emerged from around the corner of the massive sand hill and a torch was shoved into Michael's face.

What de fuck? said Michael, turning away to avoid the glare.

Calm dan paddy, said one of the soldiers.

Grand night now lads, said Kavanagh.

Yeah paddy, it's facking lavely, said the other soldier, and they continued on up into the cut.

How in de name a Jaysus did dose useless cunts end up rulin us for four hundred years? asked Kavanagh.

It's a simple matter of numbers, said Michael, more a dem dan us.

126

The road held tight to the contour of the mound and they followed it around and came to the short tunnel that served as an entrance into the enclosure. The giant guard called O'Reilly was inside the tunnel. He was stooping and doing a little jig in his rubber boots to keep himself warm.

Rough night down dere tonight lads? he said, with a shiver, and he searched Kavanagh and Michael for matches.

A bit lively alright, said Kavanagh, she cleared up nice though, and I reckon we might even be in for a bit of an indian summer.

O'Reilly was primed for delivery of his own very particular opinion on this subject. He was denied his opportunity. The door of the nearest building flew outwards and a foreman stumbled backwards onto the concrete step followed by a line of workers who came out after him all swearing and shouting and spitting. One of them was Earls. They spoke all at once, each one yelling louder than the other.

Yez can't all talk at de same time, said the foreman, so they took turns at berating him.

The most vocal was a Dublin man who stood directly in front of the foreman with his finger shoved into his face.

Don't ye bleedin talk down ta uzz mista, shouted the Dublin man, and he drew his right shoulder back as if he were preparing to throw a punch.

Go azzy boy, warned the foreman, dere's no point in gettin tick with me.

The Dublin man squared up to the foreman.

No one's gettin tick, he said, we've gaw a genuine grievance here.

One of the Wexford men demanded to speak to the Captain, the overseer of all the nitro houses.

He's busy, said the foreman.

Ah, said another of the men, he's always busy.

127

Ye can talk to em at de end of de shift, said the foreman.

What's de problem lads?

The men all turned to look into the darkness and the Captain appeared like a ghost out of the shadows.

He removed his black peaked hat, ruffled this silver crown and replaced his hat.

We want more money, said the Dublin man, das de problem.

Faster, faster, one of the workers was saying over and over, always faster.

Ye want fah-sta, said the Dublin man, well ye'll have ta pay for fah-sta.

De quicker we work de more dangerous it becomes, said a Wexford man.

Lads, lads, lads, said the Captain, and he beckoned the men away from the building and the dangerous explosives inside.

The men shuffled after him begrudgingly and gathered under a flickering electric lamp suspended from a pole by the tunnel.

Michael studied the man's face. Forty years at sea had transformed it into an intricate map of broken veins and deep wrinkles, and it had also prepared him well for his current occupation. He was composed to the point of appearing indifferent. A closer inspection however revealed eyes that were intelligent and alert. And he was an attentive overseer who was very wary of any discord or anxiety among those around him. All this was housed securely inside the body of a bull. Michael doubted he could ever attain such inner or outer strength. If he could acquire a fraction of this man's resilience that would be something.

Right, said the Captain, and am I to take it dat you have been anointed de official spokesman for yer fellow workers?

Yip, said the Dublin man emphatically.

Union man up dere in de big schmoke were ye? enquired the foreman.

I was, said the Dublin man.

No unions here yet, said the foreman.

Dere comin.

Mister Chamberlain's not too keen on organised labour, said the Captain.

Dat's his problem.

I suppose it is, said the Captain, I don't agree with Mister Chamberlain anyway. I have me own views on de subject.

Oh yeah, and what might dey be? asked the Dublin man.

Dis isn't de time or de place, said the Captain, but yev been asked ta increase de amount of nitro produced and ye want more money, fair enough, I'll speak ta Mister Cocking and see if he can get you lads a couple of bob more.

The Dublin man rubbed the back of his neck.

Yer not fobbin uz off are ye?

Look, said the Captain, I don't care how much you lads get paid, if yer happy and get on with yer work den I'm happy.

The Dublin man's anger was now almost deflated.

Why don't you lads go and take a half-hour break, said the Captain, and they trooped off through the tunnel.

The last man was Earls.

What de fuck are you gwakin at? said Earls to Michael, and he made a step forward to confront Micheal.

But Kavanagh sprang at him and took a hold of his arm with his long, thin fingers. He was squeezing Earls' arm with such force that Earls was completely paralysed with the pain.

Look now, said Kavanagh, I don't want my co-workers bein upset, and he increased the pressure a little and waited for Earls to submit.

Alright, said Earls, just let go a me.

I will indeed, said Kavanagh, and the Wexford man was released.

Off with ye, said Kavanagh, back to yer buddies like a good chap, and Earls followed the rest of the men.

If I need yer help I'll ask, said Michael.

Just go home, said Kavanagh.

I'm stayin right where I am, said Michael.

Look, said Kavanagh, by de time dat tank gets filled yer shift 'll be over so go on, off with ye.

If dat's de case, I'll go, said Michael.

It's Saturday, said Kavanagh, have a rest and go out and have a bit a fun.

A shaft of blue light floated above Michael's head projecting moving pictures onto the slightly sagging screen. It was a comedy reel of Charlie Chaplin but it was so badly worn that in places it looked like a torrent of rain. Michael didn't care. He was content not to be in the pub listening to endless disputes over the factory and whether to strike for more money. Then everything stopped. The strange machine that performed the magic of bringing the photographs to life broke down and the hall was left in near darkness. Michael glanced up at the corrugated roof. It was a tell-tale sign of the building's past. The Electric Picture Palace was in fact a converted barn previously inhabited by pigs and chickens. While Michael reflected upon this trivial bit of history the people around him were growing restless and irritated. They were getting up from their seats and leaving. Michael was glad to see the people go. He could sit alone in the dreamy black void and think. But a few people remained at the back, all of them young men with their girlfriends taking advantage of the dark to do what they were not permitted to do in daylight.

Now the film was rolling once more. This time it was a newsreel of the civilian army on the screen. He saw men and women toiling in factories and in forests and fields, hammering hot steel, felling enormous trees, sawing timber and sowing seeds. He saw trains carrying great loads and gigantic ships being built. Here was the whole of human endeavour, all dedicated to one supreme task, destruction and death. He remembered seeing the news of the explosion at the munitions factory in Silvertown near Woolwich. Fifty tonnes of TNT went up, killing seventy-three people. Nitroglycerine was even more dangerous. You didn't even need to ignite it. And Jimmy was rejoicing over the extra few bob he was going to get. We're gonna be rich, he said. It's a great opportunity ta turn a good shillin, dis factory won't be here forever, he said. They were the words of a stupid man. Rich indeed, for a day or two, until his wife got her hands on his wages and drank it. She was just as bad as Michael's father. No amount of scolding or cajoling could dissuade her from the bottle. And what was Michael going to do with a few extra shillins? Buy some new collars and another pair of shiny boots for Saturday night and Sunday morning. He sniffed the pungent ointment the nurse had given him and ran his finger along the line on his gums. The doctor was right. The factory was killing him. He knew it all along he just couldn't admit it to himself. He considered it a kind of weakness of his body. And what would he do then, if it was true, if he couldn't work in the factory? While he pondered this another far more distressing thought was demanding his attention. As soon as it came to light he was almost disappointed at the familiar nature of the problem. It was the fear, the fear of sudden death, of being blown to pieces. He had tried repeatedly to negotiate with it in his head. The only remedy was a good drink. This never failed. But he needed increasing quantities of the stuff to cut through it, and now he couldn't tolerate any quantity of drink at all without being violently sick.

Most of the men shied away from the subject of death and danger. They drank their pints to stave it off and kept it from rising up inside them. Still it sat in their bellies like a rock, a heavy indigestible load they carried with them everywhere. They lived with it every single day and hour. It never went away. They brought it home to their families, their beds, their dreams. Their nerves were worn to a thread. He saw big men, strong men, go black around the eyes. Their teeth went grey and they couldn't breath because the rot was in their lungs.

Michael came out of his mental wanderings. A gang of young revellers came in off the Main Street. Among them was Rose and her new boyfriend, Earls. Michael had seen them earlier. Somehow, with tremendous force of will, he had put them out of his mind. Now he could hear Rose's distinctive rusty voice at the back of the picture house. She was talking and giggling very loudly. She wanted to hurt him, and it did hurt him deeply, especially seeing her with Earls. And for all that he knew he would have her back in a second if she offered. Of course she would be nothing only trouble. Better that, he reasoned, than being stuck with a timid farmer's daughter or some *Holy Mary Mother a God* making oaths and the sign of the cross every five minutes.

He could leave the town. It was the only way to be free of her. The idea had never really occurred to him until Seanee's accident. The notion had grown gradually like a seed, and the more he thought about it the more he realised that there was nothing to prevent his going. He was young, without responsibility, unshackled. He could fly away and never come back. Apart from his father, no one would really care.

The gang of revellers was moving on now, probably to the nearest watering hole. Michael waited until they had left before getting up from his seat. He felt sick and dizzy. He stumbled onto the Main Street. He toppled forward and was falling towards the hard pavement.

Two strong hands took a hold of him. It was Thomas.

Are ye alright dere? he asked, and he set Michael on his feet.

132

He was with several young men and women all dressed up for the night.

Michael was unable to reply. A sharp pain was shooting down his arm and his skin had turned pale and sticky.

Thomas' friends were moving away.

I've had a few pints, this was Michael's excuse.

A few too many, said Thomas.

Yeah, said Michael, and he asked Thomas where he and his friends were off to.

We're goin ta de Royal for a slap up meal.

So dat's why yer all got up like peacocks.

Aren't we de height of sophistication, said Thomas, and he swept his new jacket back and put his hand on his hip.

Yer quare smart alright.

Dat's de way dey do it in London, said Thomas, snazzed up and eightin out.

Michael cast a sharp eye at Thomas' companions.

They were edging further and further away, except for one pretty girl who stayed at Thomas' side and was tugging at his arm and muttering that they had to leave.

For feck's sake woman will ye wait, he said, can't ye see I'm tryin ta talk ta me friend?

Huh, said the girl, and she went and stood a small distance away.

Michael straightened himself up. The pain was easing.

Yer woman's abandonin ye, he said.

She won't be goin too far, explained Thomas, I'm payin.

De sea has done ye a world a good, said Michael.

It certainly has, said Thomas, I've a few quid in me pocket. I can tank yer auld fella for dat.

He's done someone some good den, said Michael.

Ta tink I was goin ta run off with Mary, said Thomas, and he laughed inwardly.

133

Michael was bending forward. The pain had returned.

Yer not lookin great boy, said Thomas.

I'm not feelin great ta tell ye de truth, said Michael, and he rubbed his arm.

Ye haven't had a drop at all have ye? said Thomas.

Not much, said Michael.

De factory? asked Thomas.

Yes, said Michael.

It's a fuck of a place, said Thomas.

I'm workin with the nitro, twenty bob a week, said Michael.

Ye should try de sea, said Thomas.

Naw, said Michael without thinking, it's not for me.

You'd be spared havin ta work with those madmen from Wexford, said Thomas, it's de nitro dat makes dem belligerent, one or two pints and dere off like firecrackers. Yer best out a dere altogether.

Yer right about dat, said Michael.

Well, I better go, said Thomas, if dis lass gets any hungrier she'll be eightin me.

Good luck, said Michael.

Good luck, said Thomas, and he and the girl went off up the Main Street, with the girl clinging to Thomas' arm as if her life depended on it.

Michael wished he'd been more polite. His words had come out gruff and charmless without him wishing them to. And he wondered why he'd been so quick to dismiss Thomas' suggestion of going to sea. It had cured Thomas of his broken heart, so it would probably cure his. And now the idea of leaving was beginning to fix itself in his mind. The fear would stop, the sickness would end, and he would be free of Rose. He had been a coward. That is what had prevented him from leaving the factory. His sister had been brave. She understood far better than he what possibilities life offered. It was all so clear to her. And already his fear was subsiding. It was replaced with feelings of excitement of the kind he hadn't experienced since he was a child. He would work in the factory until he found a place on one of the ships. The sea had its dangers too and if it didn't suit him he would try something else and something else until he found a trade that he liked. He imagined a great adventure and he could put away quite a tidy sum if he refrained from spending frivolously. He could save a little nest egg. On his return he would find a decent girl, not like the ones he had chased after in the past. And finally, after such a long time the torment lifted. He was at peace with himself, and as he walked in the fading light a contented smile decorated his face.

CHAPTER 14

Another large bottle please Mister Burke, said Michael's father.

The publican scrutinized his customer. He wondered if he could afford it. Michael's father had been perched in the same spot every afternoon for the past week and the publican was sure his money or his body would give out soon.

I knows what yer tinkin, said Michael's father, rattling his coins, and there it was, yet another shilling was placed on the counter.

Ye might spare a taut for yer finances, said the publican, or yer liver.

Yer absolutely right, said Michael's father, and I'll be addressing dose points in due course.

I'm very glad ta hear it, said the publican, in a slow, joyless drone.

In de meantime however, said Michael's father, ye can continue plyin me with whatever flavour of poison I wish.

If you say so, said the publican, and he took the shilling and dutifully replaced it with a drink and some change.

To yer good health, said Michael's father.

Tanks a million, said the publican, and he watched his customer as he rifled impatiently through the pages of the *Wicklow Newsletter*.

Dat's what I'm looking for, said Michael's father, and he lay the paper down on the bar.

His index finger commenced to follow the text of a large advert.

LOANS TO CLERGYMEN, PROFESSIONALS AND TRADESMEN, DISCRETION GUARANTEED, EASY PAYMENTS

I'd hardly call you a professional now, said the publican.

I'm a tradesman, am I not? said Michael's father.

Yer not doing much trade today, said the publican.

De business needs some investment, said Michael's father.

The publican laughed to himself. It was well know that Michael's father bought no stock, he paid no creditors, and while every other establishment on the Main Street prospered the number of his customers quickly dwindled. The few that did come did so out of a sense of loyalty to Michael's mother. But even they had no desire to deal with an unreasonable and unreliable drunkard, and eventually, after numerous quarrels, every last one of them took their money elsewhere. So the shop that had flourished when their mother was alive shut its doors as tightly as the lid on her coffin and all hope of its reopening was buried under six feet of earth.

And with the aid of dis loan, continued Michael's father.

Huh, said the publican, what would you be needin a loan for anyway? Sure yev plenty of money ta throw away on porter.

Well now, explained Michael's father, with a heavy grimace, it's not…

It's not what?

It's not my money exactly, said Michael's father.

Ye mean ye stole it? asked the publican, who was extremely eager to find out where all the shillings were coming from.

I did actually, said Michael's father, with a very peculiar laugh.

This was more sarcasm than the grumpy publican could tolerate and he went up into the private quarters above the bar where he and his wife lived. No sanctuary was to be found in his wife's company either. There was the thud of the publican's large feet on the low ceiling, and without any warning Michael's father heard a quarrel break out between them. This fierce exchange was interrupted by the banging of furniture and the demise of some crockery. Then a door slammed and the publican's wife came tearing down the stairs. Michael's father shifted in his stool to see up the corridor. She was taking a coat from a line of hooks. The woman was so enraged she couldn't find the sleeve inside the garment and had to take a moment to calm herself. Once the coat was on she stopped and debated with herself whether to take if off and go back upstairs.

I'm goin out, she shouted to her husband.

She waited briefly, hoping for a reply and an opportunity to make up. She got none and so she left, closing the door behind her with such force that the whole building shook.

When the publican returned his face was transformed from his usual pink complexion to a crimson red that set his ears on fire.

The two men said nothing for a long while. The empty bar seemed to fill up with the sound of silence disturbed only by the odd horse and cart passing by. After the argument with his wife the publican was content to enjoy this peace and tranquillity. His customer however was more inclined to talking than quiet contemplation and after ten minutes he piped up.

Isn't it a strange thing, he said.

Isn't what strange? asked the publican, merely to humour his drunken customer.

Dat I am here and you're dere for precisely de same reason, said Michael's father.

And what would dat be? asked the publican, and he lit a cigarette and spat a tiny bit of tobacco onto the floor.

Women, said Michael's father, bloody women, and his hand came down on the counter so hard the publican jumped.

You see, said Michael's father triumphantly.

You see what? asked the publican.

Yer not denying it are you?

I'm not denyin what? asked the publican, and he drew hard on the his fag.

Yer here because of your wife, said Michael's father, why else would a man who hates being behind a bar be dere in the first place?

Who says I hate it? said the publican.

Ah now, said Michael's father, ye do yer level best to hide it, sure I've been dere meself, years I've spent behind de counter in dat damn shop, and he pointed his thumb in the general direction of his deceased wife's now defunct establishment.

I make a livin, said the publican, defending himself.

So did I, said Michael's father, still, I wager it gives ye no pleasure in dispensing dis most common of weaknesses, and he raised his bottle.

No! I can't say it does, said the publican.

Yev simply ended up in de same line of business as yer in-laws, said Michael's father.

The publican looked around to make sure his wife hadn't returned.

Dere's some truth in what you're saying, he replied.

Go on, said Michael's father, no need to hold back.

So the normally tight-lipped publican let his defenses slip and in his frustration he revealed that it was indeed true, that he never wanted to work in a bar, that he had been persuaded against his own wishes to please his wife.

It's me very own story, said Michael's father, in every essential detail.

139

Is it indeed? said the publican, with some excitement, and amid this stir of emotions Michael father enticed the publican to have a drink.

No, said the publican resolutely, stubbing out his half-smoked fag.

Ah come on outta dat, said Michael's father, a drink to mark de end of our bondage, just a little one.

De end of yer bondage perhaps, not mine, said the publican, suddenly dejected.

Well to mine den.

I couldn't.

And why not?

I never drink when I'm workin.

Don't ye owe it ta yerself, said Michael's father, for twenty years doin somethin agin yer own nature and instinct and for what? Just to keep her in dere quiet. And ye see de thanks ye get.

Best not to, said the publican.

The publican had good reason for his abstinence. He had witnessed the bar room confessional at first hand many times.

But Michael's father was not giving up easily.

Ah now, he said, finishing off his own drink, a small reward, who would begrudge it, no one, not for all dose years.

The publican peeked into the corridor leading to his private quarters, there was no sign of his wife.

Who could argue against dat logic, said Michael's father.

Who indeed, said the publican, and eventually he forgot his own golden rule and he poured himself a generous shot of precious whiskey. Unfortunately he was not much of a drinker. The strong liquor went straight to his head and it wasn't long before he was engulfed in self pity.

I wanted to go up ta Maynooth and be a scholar, he said, almost tearfully.

And ye would've been a great scholar too I bet, said Michael's father, I had big plans meself, I was off to Australia, a land of opportunity, if it wasn't for gettin married and saddling meself with two children.

The men went on in this vein complaining about how their women had hampered their progress, and they had plenty of steam in them, a lifetime of resentment was going to take some time to exorcise.

Would ye listen ta the two of them, interjected a voice from down the corridor.

It was the publican's wife. She was at the bottom of the stairs. They had no idea how long she had been there. However long it was, she had clearly grasped the full gist of their conversation. She removed her coat, put it on the hook and advanced like a bull up the corridor and into the bar.

Would you kindly leave? she said.

I was only messin, said Michael's father, attempting to charm the woman.

The publican however knew from experience that there would be no appealing to his wife and he refrained from contradicting his wife or offering support to his new friend.

Yer a blasted troublemaker, said the publican's wife.

I've no idea what de blazes yer on about, said Michael's father.

Go on, get out, screamed the publican's wife in a tone so shrill that Michael's father immediately withdrew to the door to lessen the effect on his ears.

Yer gettin yerself into an awful state over notin, he said, I was only messing I tell ye.

The publican's wife was filling her lungs for another outburst so Michael's father quickly spun on his heels and left.

CHAPTER 15

Catherine was staring out of her bedroom window. Mary was in the back garden playing with the boy. Mary glanced upwards. The phone was ringing for the third time, and Catherine refused to answer it.

She was annoyed to see Mary still outside with the child. She had asked the girl to take him to the beach and not to return until at least six o'clock. She was incapable of following the simplest of requests. It was no surprise. Catherine's mother-in-law had employed the girl because she was cheap. She had only ever worked selling vegetables in her family's little shop somewhere in the town and packing boxes in the factory. The girl had no experience as a maid in a decent household. Her clothes were shabby and her shoes had holes in them. She might as well have had a field hand or a ploughman working for her. Of course the girl was completely without culture. She had never read a book in her life. Catherine could almost forgive her that. What could you expect, with a father who was seen drunk on the Main Street every other day.

What she found most offensive however was Mary's indifference to her own ignorance. When Catherine complimented her on her little drawings the girl got into a huff. It was as if she was trying to convert the silly girl to another religion. Sometimes she saw Mary looking at her as if she were an oddity in a museum. She had no doubt heard the stories and the gossip in her mother-in-law's house and was probably convinced her employer was mad.

The old woman had employed Mary to look after the boy. She didn't trust her daughter-in-law to care for her precious grandson. The old woman imagined it was punishment for Catherine not being nearly good enough. Catherine didn't mind at all. It wasn't her child anyway. She might have loved it more if it were her own, but it wasn't, and the boy preferred Mary's company anyway. Catherine didn't protest, it left her free to paint. Of course the old woman objected to her daughter-in-law being a painter. It was harlotry for a woman to pursue the life of an artist, she said, and she often withheld money for Catherine's painting materials. The old woman took her on shopping trips to Dublin instead to buy expensive clothes she didn't want. To be happy you must be beautiful, the old woman said. And when they weren't shopping Catherine was advised to pass her time gardening. The house had a beautiful garden, according to her mother-in-law. The old woman wasn't going to say otherwise, she had picked the house for her son. Catherine had no say in it. She had no money. She was a silent partner in the proceedings. It was less than three hundred yards from the old woman's front door. Close enough to keep a watchful eye, or so the old woman thought. It was no deterrent to Oscar. He said it made his nocturnal visits more exciting. But there would be no more visits.

The phone was ringing again. It was Oscar. He didn't have the courage to tell her to her face.

Mary was at the bottom of the stairs asking if she should pick it up.

Catherine shouted through the door. It's not important, she said, and Mary did as she was told and went away.

Catherine refused to speak to him. She couldn't bear to hear what he was going to say. It would break her completely, push her over the edge and plunge her back into her madness. It had already started, the headaches, the bewildered irritation, and the nightmares. They were always about her husband. The night

143

before she dreamt he was at her front door, a bedraggled unshaven mess, his clothes filthy, a pistol in his trembling hand. She was tormented with guilt. She wasn't sure why. She had married him because he had promised to look after her, and he had brought her to this awful place, to cure her he said, and to get her away from the war. Or was it to be rid of her, to leave her in the care of his mother while he went to France. And now she was a prisoner in her own house with nowhere to go and not a single companion. So he couldn't blame her for seeking out affection. If he wasn't there to give it she had to go elsewhere. And who would she turn to when Oscar had deserted her? No one, there was no one else. If only they had stayed in Dublin. They had a good life there until her husband had changed, everything had changed. Then the war broke out. That was when she had tried to kill herself by jumping out a window.

So the decision was made. Her husband wished to return to his family home and she agreed, she had no income of her own and was bound to him. It would be better for her, he said, she would be away from the war. But it wasn't as he had promised. The war was everywhere. She told herself it wasn't but how could she deny the horrible factory that manufactured death right outside her bedroom window? How could she erase the smell and the smoke and the workers marching in the middle of the bleak winter nights long before the sun could be bothered to show itself? And there were the young soldiers in the barracks next door. It was like a cruel joke. In the whole of Ireland could a worse place have been found? Then her husband said he was going to France to help in one of the hospitals near the front. He was abandoning his wife, and his son. The summer and Oscar saved her. If they hadn't come along she would have drowned herself in the sea. She started to paint. She painted the marching men and the soldiers slumped against the pillar of the barracks, she painted the sky and the sea and factory. It was only a respite, a break in the never-ending black cloud that followed her everywhere.

A motorcar was out on the road. It stopped near the house and the engine was turned off. Catherine went out onto the landing. There was a knock at the front door. Mary ran from the garden to answer it.

Leave it, said Catherine.

She told Mary to go back to the garden and she went to the boy's room at rear of the house. The room was chilly. It was more like a hotel chamber than a child's bedroom. The fire was never lit. The boy rarely slept there. He preferred to be in his grandmother's house where there was an endless supply of cakes and he could make as much noise as he wished.

Catherine closed the bedroom door, drew the curtains over and sat on the tiny bed. The knocking continued. It was more insistent. Catherine blocked it out. She was very cold. She took the quilt from the bed and wrapped it around herself. A slim shaft of light found its way through the break in the curtains. The narrow beam cut across her lap. She looked at the design on the quilt. She had never noticed it before. There were lots of colourful soldiers embroidered into squares. She began to study them intensely and lapsed into a daydream until she was disturbed by a noise. The boy was in the bedroom. He was looking for something. Catherine stood up quickly and the quilt fell to the floor. The banging had ceased. It was replaced by the sound of the engine starting up. The boy couldn't find his jumper and he was asking Catherine to help. Catherine told him to ask Mary and she went to landing window. She caught a glimpse of the motorcar as it began to descend the hill. As it disappeared it let out an enormous bang from the exhaust. It was louder than a gunshot and a horse coming out of the barracks was so startled that it reared up in a panic, dislodged its mount and threw him to the ground.

145

Four soldiers came rushing out the gates and were helping the man.

He was in de house.

Catherine looked down. The boy was behind her and he was pointing.

Who was in de house?

The boy's arm fell to his side and he moved away.

Catherine repeated the question.

Who was in de house?

The boy withered at her interrogation.

Who..was..in..de..house?

Catherine was looming over him. Her tight grip was on his shoulders and she was shaking him.

De soldier with de blond hair, said the boy.

Where in de house was he?

Where was he in de house? she asked a second time.

He was in de kitchen, the boy blurted out.

Catherine took the boy by the arm and hauled him down the stairs.

Mary was at the sideboard with her back to Catherine. In front of her was an open bottle of whiskey.

What de blazes are ye doin? said Catherine.

I'm a bit under de weather, she explained, and she replaced the cork.

So ye just help yerself to my husband's whiskey?

I didn't mean any harm, said Mary, I just needed a little shot to give me strength.

I'm de one dat needs to be given strength, said Catherine, and she placed both her hands on her chest to calm herself.

Are ye alright? said Mary.

James told me a soldier was in the kitchen, said Catherine, and she tugged at the little boy's hand to prompt him.

He was unable to speak.

146

Tell her what ye said, Catherine shrieked.

The boy winced and pushed his thighs together. He wanted to pee desperately.

He found de neighbour's dog down on de beach, said Mary, and he was returnin it, dat's all.

James said you were kissin him in de kitchen.

He came in without bein asked, said Mary.

You were kissin some soldier in my house, in my kitchen.

He forced himself upon me, said Mary, he was drunk, I swear to God, on my mother's soul Mrs O'Connell, I swear.

He wasn't drunk was he? said Catherine to the boy.

The boy's eyes were welling up and he was going to pee on himself.

Yer frightenin him, said Mary, and she knelt down and wiped the boy's tears away.

I didn't invite him in did I? said Mary.

The boy couldn't breathe. The air was trapped in his lungs and he was choking.

It's not important, said Mary, it's not important, stop cryin now, stop cryin.

Go outside, said Catherine to the boy, and he ran out into the garden and went behind a bush to pee.

I won't put up with...dat sort a carry on in my house, said the doctor's wife.

On me fader's life, said Mary, crossing herself, I never asked dat soldier in here.

Get out, said Catherine.

But, but ye don't understand, pleaded Mary, dat bastard, he tried to rape me. I'd never lie about such a ting.

Go, said Catherine.

Mary went out into the hall, removed her apron and put her coat on. She was going to cry, she wouldn't allow herself.

The key, said Catherine,

147

Mary took the key from her coat pocket. She didn't want to hand it over.

Catherine plucked it from her palm.

I'll send yer money on, she said.

Mary simply nodded as she fastened the buttons on her old coat.

I just can't put up with such indecent behaviour, said Catherine.

Indecent behaviour, repeated Mary, ye bloody hypocrite.

Catherine was speechless at the outburst. For months the girl had hardly said a word, little or nothing was heard out of her, and now this sudden violence.

Goodbye, said Mary, and she slammed the door behind her.

Mary walked quickly along the footpath. She was in a rage and was talking loudly to herself.

Kick me out, she said, I couldn't give a damn, I'm goin ta England, ta London actually, I bet you would like ta go dere wouldn't ye Mrs O'Connell. Well I've got money. I've saved every penny I could. I haven't got a lot but I've got enough. Ye see dese auld shoes I'm wearing Mrs bloody O'Connell, dat yer always lookin at because dey've got holes in dem. Well I could've bought another pair. I could've bought another five pairs if it pleased me, I didn't though, I kept me money. And who was she to be talkin about people doin indecent tings when all de time de phone was ringin and her lover was callin. Did she take her for a fool? Did she tink dat she was blind and hadn't notice de tall grass at de back of de garden trodden flat or de stink a fags in de mornin and de whiskey bottle dat was emptyin and miraculously fillin itself up every week. Indecent, indecent! De nerve of de woman. She should've boxed her face. De bitch went ridin around in dat motorcar with her boyfriend where all de world could see, while her skivvy had been discreet, said notin to no one and pretended to herself dat notin was goin on. And now

148

de bloody woman was in a state because she'd been dumped. De woman was mad and she was gonna be a whole lot madder when her boyfriend was gone. Poor jealous cow, dere was more to life dan de attentions of men. And what kind of a victory was it, receiving de affections of dis fella? He was only playin with her and keepin himself amused. He was flirtin with all with de girls in de factory. He was very popular, according to Michael. And if Mrs O'Connell thought she was de only one bein taken out in dat motorcar well she was very much mistaken. Wasn't he out last Sunday in dat fancy contraption with a pretty ting from de laboratory in de factory.

Are ye alright Mary?

Mrs Dempsey was sitting out on her doorstep smoking a fag.

Mary had passed her neighbour without even seeing her.

Yer in another world luvee.

What? said Mary.

Yer talkin to yerself, said Mrs Dempsey.

Oh sorry Mrs Dempsey, said Mary.

Mary was searching for her key. Then she fumbled putting it in the lock.

The house was empty. She raced up the stairs to her room, threw back the rug and prised up the floorboard with the two funny knots with the end of her key. She removed the old tea tin with the pretty picture on the lid that had been in the family for years.

Mary didn't take off the lid. Something wasn't right. She tested the weight then rattled the contents. The tin should have been full, it was almost half empty.

Oh, Jaysus, she screamed, how could ye do dat me? And the tin fell from her hand and the precious coins went everywhere.

CHAPTER 16

Mary was waiting by the gates of the factory. She was at the end of her shift. Several young women had gathered nearby and were gawking at her and gossiping. The most boisterous was the woman called Rose. Mary paid them no heed. She turned instead to the laboratory just inside the gates where the English women and men were employed testing all the chemicals. She could see through the large windows into the building. Mary envied them. It was clean and bright, and quiet. Most of all she envied the quiet. She had returned to her old job and back to the very employment she dreaded more than any she could imagine, filling cartridges with gelatine. And just like before, her entire day was occupied on her knees feeding the awful machine that made the endless clanking noise.

She leaned forward, raised her dress and rubbed her legs. Her hands were rough from the explosive powder and her skin caught in the stitches of her stockings. It was difficult to endure, but Mary knew that she must endure it. Adversity will make ye stronger, that's what her mother had told her. The other girls were stupid anyway. Their jobs and their little bit of independence would soon vanish and few of them realized it. Back they would go to their farms and villages and remote towns in the wilderness of the Wicklow hills, their money all spent.

The chatter of the women grew more animated. A well dressed man was coming their way. The younger women wriggled in the hope of a complimentary glance. They were all disappointed. He headed not towards them but towards Mary.

Hello, he said cautiously.

Mary didn't wish to reply.

It's Oscar, he said, Mrs O'Connell's friend.

I know who ye are sir, said Mary.

Are ye waitin for someone? he asked.

Me brother, said Mary, and her stern gaze fixed itself upon some distant nothing.

Then she remembered the day on the quay when he had helped her, for that she owed him some courtesy at least, so she conceded a question.

So what are ye doin here? she asked.

I'm now employed by the Kynoch Explosives Company as a lowly clerk, he said, and you?

Filling cartridges, said Mary, and the thought of it made her scratch her hands.

I'd swop my job for yours any day, said Oscar.

The comment passed from his lips so lightly, and it angered Mary. Look at me hands, that's what she wanted to say. Ye tink it's noble ta do dis kinda work? Dat's what she wanted to ask him. And why did he hate his job? Because it was boring, or maybe he found it degrading having to work at all.

She held it all back.

Instead she enquired about Mrs O'Connell. The question was intended to have a sting. His reward for his foolishness.

Oscar tugged at his new starched collar and then his index finger followed a deep crease in his brow.

Mary had struck right at his heart and it gave her a rush of malevolent pleasure. His pain passed quickly however and after a flash of resignation it evaporated.

I haven't seen her in a while, said Oscar, and he offered her a cigarette from the packet in his hand.

Mary looked down her nose at what was being presented to her.

Yer alright, she said.

Oscar slid one out of the box with his thumb to entice her further.

Oh, I'm sorry, he said, perhaps ye don't want ta smoke in public.

Are ye patronisin me?

No, no, said Oscar.

Go on, give us one den.

He struck his last remaining match gracefully and lit her cigarette. The sweet smell of his cologne and the odour of expensive tobacco wafted against her face.

I suppose yer angry at her, said Oscar, and I can't blame ye for that.

I didn't do anytin wrong, she said, she only did it because-

She was coughing on the smoke. Oscar gave her a moment to recover herself.

Because what? he asked.

Mary refused to answer.

Ye shouldn't judge her too harshly though, he said, she's very lonely.

Now it was Mary's turn to be stabbed in the heart.

We're all lonely, retorted Mary.

Oscar nodded and relented.

We appear to have an audience, he said, and he pointed discreetly at the women loitering at the gate.

Mary flicked the ash clumsily.

Dey'll tink I'm corrupting ye, said Oscar.

I couldn't give a damn what dey tink, said Mary, and she puffed away on the cigarette until it was a stub.

Oscar offered her another.

Mary spotted Michael approaching.

Dere he is, she said, and she plucked the cigarette deftly from the packet and dropped it into her satchel.

Well good bye den, said Oscar.

Good bye, said Mary.

What are dey starin at?

Mary swung her brother round so his back was to the women.

If dey were men dey'd be straight off ta de pub, said Mary.

Yer one ta talk, said Michael, and the fresh pink flesh on Mary's cheeks changed to a scalding shade of red.

I've no idea what yer talkin about, said Mary indignantly to hide her shame.

Jaysus, said Michael, ye can still raise a bit of colour, dere can't be many of dem left in ye.

I'm just a bit hot dat's all, said Mary.

Look, said Micheal, dere's no harm in a little drop now and den.

If ye say so, said Mary, and she gestured for him to hand over his pay packet.

Michael gave it without objection and he received a few bob back as pocket money. The act seemed strange, demeaning even, and yet it was comforting. In his own hands these hard-earned shillings would disappear like sand through his fingers. His sister on the other hand could be trusted not to spend it, and would only relinquish it when there was good reason to.

What's this? asked Mary.

Michael was holding out a small box for his sister to take.

Don't tell me, said Mary, ye bought it for her over dere?

Tempted as he was, Michael couldn't bring himself to lie.

I did, he said, but I won't be doin such a ting again.

Mary flipped the lid open, tutted and let it snap closed.

What use would I have for a fancy ring? she said.

I was tinkin you could sell it, said Michael, it's worth a bit, and ye'll get more for it dan I could.

We can share the money, said Mary.

153

Grand, said Michael, and he put his arm around his sister and gave her a kiss.

We'll be alright, he said.

We will, she said, and she began to cry.

What's all dat about? asked Michael.

I miss Ma, she said, and I miss Thomas.

I miss her too, said Michael.

Here, said Mary, and she removed the red scarf she was wearing and she placed it tightly around his neck.

Micheal began undoing the dainty little knot Mary had tied.

I'm not wearin dat yoke, I'll look like a girl.

And who's gonna be lookin at ye, protested Mary, and she retied the knot.

It does get chilly before de dawn alright, he admitted.

Precisely, sure dat's why I'm giving it to ye.

Tanks, he said.

Michael took the long straight road parallel to the perimeter of the factory. He was early for his shift and he walked at a gentle pace. The reconciliation with his sister had calmed his nerves and his spirit sat much more easily with the world than it had in a long time. The familiar black pit in his stomach would return when he reached his destination, but his plans for the future had cheered him greatly, and the idea of some great adventure had entered his head and would not be dislodged.

He came around a gentle bend in the road and he heard something rustling behind him. Oscar was climbing out from behind a thick bush. He was caught in the tangle of branches. He was also buttoning up his trousers and an unlit cigarette was dangling from his mouth. Michael was watching him with some amusement. Once he'd freed himself from the vegetation and the matter of his trousers was attended to, he ran after Michael, his pockets jingle-jangling with change.

He called out to Michael.

Excuse me, he said, and he waved his cigarette.

Do you have some fire? he asked.

I do, said Michael, do you have a fag?

Oscar drew close and produced a cigarette from a box.

Michael immediately recognised the man standing before him. Oscar was also familiar with the person now lighting his cigarette and it put him on his guard. But he was not the aggressive individual Oscar had met before. The signs of violence, the bruised knuckles and the little black hole where his front tooth used to reside, were still there. The bristling anger however was gone. Oscar was amazed at the transformation. His whole countenance had changed to such a degree that had it not been for his missing tooth he might have been someone else altogether. It was as if he had been exorcised. The raging demon had been expelled, cast out of him. He was no doubt free of the temptress who'd been toying so recklessly with his affections, and as Oscar looked upon the young man he felt an instant attachment and affection to him that was so contrary to his earlier encounter he could hardly believe it.

The cigarette was lit and Michael waited for Oscar to move on. He didn't. He asked Michael if he was walking to the Spion Kop.

I am sir, said Michael.

Well, I'll join you for a bit, said Oscar, and he hesitated, if ye don't mind dat is?

Yer more dan welcome sir, said Michael.

Are you Mary's brother? asked Oscar.

I am, said Michael, and yer Mrs O'Connell's friend?

You saw dat terrible explosion in de dryin house, said Oscar.

I did sir, said Michael, and I had a very lucky escape, me friend Seanee wasn't so fortunate.

No, said Oscar, and the two men refrained from speaking for a bit as a mark of respect.

And yer still workin here, said Oscar, dat's courageous.

Not for much longer, said Michael, I'm goin ta sea.

Huh, said Oscar, yer a very lucky boy.

Michael could see a genuine yearning in the man now walking by his side. He'd seen the same longing in so many other men who could never leave the factory. Some were too old. Others were bound to their wives and children. What bound this man however was his class. He was spoilt and made soft by privilege. The sea was no place for him. He was made for the pursuit of leisure. He would probably inherit a lot of money one day and live a better life than Michael ever would. Michael thought no less of the man for it. Such was the order of things. That was the way fortunes were divided.

The road was rising up and it revealed a scattering of buildings. Just beyond them was the cold, black sea. The two men looked out over the panorama and we're pleased with what they saw. Immense as the factory was it could not diminish the beauty they were now witnessing. This was Oscar's only compensation. This strange exotic landscape of sand dunes and the closeness of the water was what made the factory tolerable.

Soon they were at the northern most gate of the factory.

I'll be leavin ye here sir, said Michael, and he gave Oscar his matches.

Tank you, said Oscar, and good luck on yer travels.

Michael joined a line of men and when his turn came he was searched and allowed to proceed. When he got to Hut Number 189 Kavanagh was waiting for him.

She's empty again, said Kavanagh, and the two men climbed up the steep path to the road and they walked around the mound to tunnel.

O'Reilly was at the far end.

Any unrest tonight? asked Kavanagh.

No, said O'Reilly, the Red Army must have taken the evenin off.

Perhaps dere'll be a revolution tomorra, said Kavanagh.

As long as it's not on my watch, said O'Reilly, and he examined both men's jackets for matches.

Where's de Captain? asked Kavangh.

Through the left tunnel, said O'Reilly, and Kavanagh and Michael passed under the electric light, through a second passageway into an adjoining mound.

Rising up in front of them was a tall, narrow structure with large sash windows and a corrugated roof. It filled the entire space within the mound and had the air of a place of confinement or punishment. Michael's instinct was to retreat. He didn't give the impulse time take hold. He moved forward impatiently and Kavanagh pulled him back and asked him if he was blind.

What? replied Michael.

Kavanagh directed his finger to a large sign.

KNOCK BEFORE ENTERING.

Michael did as the notice instructed and they went inside.

The building was much the same as the hut where he and Kavanagh mixed the guncotton and nitro. Apart from the fixtures it was stripped clean of tools and furniture of any kind. The floor was timber and lined with lead. The walls consisted of rough planks. The internal structure was made entirely of bare timber. The floor above, which was really a raised platform, had timber railings and was held up with thick square timber posts. The building was illuminated by a series of bulbs that gave out a pitiful dim light. Above this paltry yellow hue were the exposed sheets of the metal roof. In the centre of the floor was an oblong ceramic tank that looked like an open sarcophagus. Two thick

157

pipes descending through the floor of the platform and fed into the coffin-like container.

Leaning against a window frame in the shadows underneath the platform was a man of about twenty years of age. His cap was pulled down over his forehead and his hands were plunged deep into his pockets to conserve the warmth of his body.

How's it goin dere? said Kavanagh.

The mysterious figure shifted his weight from one leg to the other, extracted a fragment of wax from his left ear, flicked it away and resumed his prolonged gaze out at the sand hill less than five feet away. Kavanagh thought little of it. It was common for men, and even women, of the town to behave with prejudice towards strangers and country people.

Kavanagh went to the foot of the stairs and called up to the Captain who was bent over and was squinting at a pressure gauge. The Captain wiped the mist off the glass, looked again at the needle and made an adjustment to the valve below. The fluid inside made a gurgling protest and the pipes shuddered. The needle responded slowly, shifting its way in little jerks in an anticlockwise direction towards zero.

Once the Captain was satisfied with the new level he switched his attention quickly to Kavanagh.

What can I do for you? he asked.

Hut 189 needs filling, said Kavanagh, in his soft, slightly wispy accent.

The Captain strained to hear and when he failed to catch what was being said a second time he told Kavanagh to come on up and to bring the apprentice with him. Kavanagh nudged Michael in the back and together they went up onto the platform.

They were now in a cramped space with their heads just below the beams. Most of the area was taken up by another tank. This particular container was more like a very large barrel. It was about chest height with a dome on top, was made of heavy steel and was held together along the seams with large rivets.

The Captain greeted Michael with great cordiality and offered his deep regret at the passing of his mother.

She was an exceptional woman, he said, and a good friend.

Michael had not anticipated this expression of sympathy and the Captain, seeing his discomfort, suggested they crack on.

This apparatus, said the Captain, is called a nitrator and inside nitric acid and glycerin are combined to make nitroglycerine.

Michael's friend Jimmy was busy manoeuvring himself around the tank checking all the other valves and gauges that controlled the flow of chemicals in and out of the nitrator.

How are ye? said Michael to his friend.

Jimmy barely responded. He was fully occupied with the task. Even with the Captain close at hand he was fearful of some miscalculation or overlooking some small detail that would lead to disaster.

Michael thought his friend singularly unsuited to the job. He was a heavy set man with fleshy shoulders and a big gut and he struggled to squeeze himself into the narrow space around the nitrator.

He's as jumpy as a rabbit, said the Captain, aside to Kavanagh and Michael.

Dat's not a bad ting now, said Kavanagh, makes a man more diligent.

The Captain smiled in agreement and he buttoned his double-breasted sailor's tunic up to his neck.

De nights are gettin cauld, said Kavanagh.

Dey are indeed, said the Captain, without much concern.

The Captain pointed and Michael peered into a porthole in the dome of the tank.

A fresh batch of nitroglycerine especially for you lads, said the Captain, and he gave Jimmy the nod to empty the load.

159

Jimmy began twisting a large wheel at the base of the tank.

It's stiff as hell dat one, said the Captain, and with good reason.

Another batch comin down, shouted Jimmy, and the man below went and stood by the oblong tank and watched the nitroglycerine pour lazily into the coffin.

In the better light Michael could see that it was Earls.

How are ye? said Earls, and he winked at Michael.

It was an obvious attempt to get a little rise out of him.

Stop fuckin around, snarled the Captain at Earls, or I'll fire your arse outta here quare quick.

Earls' jaw tightened as if he was chewing on something tough.

The Captain's body went limp and his head fell to one side. It was an invitation for Earls to speak and confront him if he wished.

Earls fidgeted with his jacket sleeves and his jaw went slack.

Good man, said the Captain sarcastically, now get on with what yer bein paid ta do.

Earls whipped out a cloth that was hanging from his back pocket, placed it over his nose and mouth and tied it in a thick knot at the back of his head.

Would ye look at Billy the Kid, said Jimmy.

Dat's me, said Earls, and made his hand into the shape of a gun, pointed it Michael and with his other hand flicked back the imaginary hammer.

Get on with it, shouted the Captain to Earls.

Earls took what looked like a very shallow shopping basket from the floor and commenced skimming the surface of the deadly liquid. He deposited what he'd collected in a separate chamber at the end of the tank. He performed this task repeatedly with considerable dexterity and speed.

The impurities sit at the top, explained the Captain, and he signalled to Jimmy to proceeded to fill the tank with the correct amount of nitric acid.

Now, said the Captain, the fun and games beings.

Michael looked to Kavanagh for an explanation.

Dere gonna add the glycerin, said Kavanagh.

Coming through the rear wall was a long, thick flexible hose. On the end of the hose was a steel nozzle with a lever on a heavy spring. Jimmy took the end of the hose from a hook, carried it to the tank, got up on a wooden box and placed it in an airtight inlet on the top of the dome. He then stood poised on the box awaiting instructions from the Captain.

On the dome of the tank was a giant thermometer about a half inch in diameter. The thermometer passed through the skin of the tank and descended all the way to the bottom. The Captain put his hands behind his back and brought his eye up to the slender glass instrument.

Go ahead Jimmy, said the Captain, nice and easy.

Jimmy pressed gingerly on the lever and the glycerin burst forth in a great gush into the tank.

She's grand, said the Captain, we've just got ta make sure de mixture doesn't overheat.

The Captain indicated a red band near the top of the thermometer.

De mercury hits dat mark, he said, and de lot could self-detonate.

What do ye do den? enquired Michael.

We dump de load into a water tank below, said the Captain.

The mercury was ascending rapidly. The Captain mimicked its ascent with his hand, as if he was willing it by the power of magic.

Jimmy's hand was trembling.

Hould her down Jimmy, said the Captain casually, and then his eyes wandered into the far corner. There was nothing there.

What? said Jimmy, what's wrong.

Whist! said the Captain.

What? repeated Jimmy.

A distant voice rose into a scream and through the window they saw the fireball rise above the ridge of the sand hill. The earth quaked and Michael was thrown backwards onto the lower floor. Jimmy was closest to the upper window. The shattered glass stripped his face to a skeleton. The Captain and Kavanagh's backs were cut to shreds. There was an almighty crash. A huge lump of concrete landed on the roof above the oblong tank. It pierced the corrugated sheet and was pressing down and tearing the thin metal. Earls didn't run. He picked Michael up and together they staggered towards the door but it refused to open. In that instant Michael knew his life was over. He was going to die. And he was so close to salvation. Then the concrete fell, the sun exploded and Michael was rising upwards at great speed inside a fireball. It was like the vapours of hell. The heat was like intense cold. It scorched all his clothes and flesh. It entered his lungs and cooked them. Up he went to a great height and then he was descending through hot, sticky smoke. He came through the smoke and into a clear night sky. The stars seemed closer and more vivid than they ever had before. He saw a small ship on the horizon. Maybe this was the ship he would have sailed away in. Now he was falling rapidly and rotating like a wheel. He hit the water and was plunged into a mass of swirling fish, and down and down and down he sank into the cold black heart of the bottomless, uncaring sea.

CHAPTER 17

Mary closed the fasteners on the bulging carpet bag and tested its weight. It was heavy and there was a long journey ahead. She went through the contents in her head. Nothing could be removed. She would just have to manage.

She took the bag and went downstairs into her brother's room. She walked around touching things lightly, trying to set them in her mind. Her fingers glided over the cold metal of the curved brass bed frame. She made a line in the dust on the oak drawers, caressed the head of the Virgin on the bedside table, peered down into the water jug on the small stand and inspected the dead spider inside. On a lonely shelf by the chimney breast was her brother's modest collection of books. She felt the worn letters on the spines and whispered the strange and exotic titles - *Alice's Adventures in Wonderland*, *Moby Dick*, *The Arabian Nights* - as if they were spells that would conjure something magical. She opened the narrow wardrobe, sniffed the mothballs and stroked his Sunday clothes.

She went into the sitting room. The chair by the fire was empty. The deep impression of her father remained. She lowered herself slowly into the tattered piece of furniture. She had always avoided using this particular seat. It was his domain. Anyone occupying it would be greeted with a sharp whistle and her father's upturned thumb. What would her father do now if he saw her sitting there?

On the mantelpiece was a sealed, addressed envelope. Inside was the letter she had written to the doctor. The letter that was

163

her revenge. The letter she couldn't bring herself to send. Her father had offered to post it. Seeing it there day after day had vexed him. Why don't ye be rid of de damn yoke, he said. He wasn't interested in the contents, it was the procrastination that bothered him.

Mary folded the letter carefully, put it in her coat pocket and left the house. A gang of young children were playing in the street. The game was a re-enactment of the explosion. The ringleader, an unruly boy of about nine, threw his arms up in the air, let out a loud bang and his playmates staggered and fell dramatically, mimicking fatal wounds. The performance was suspended as Mary passed. The children somehow sensed they were doing something wrong. Mary wasn't upset. They were too young to understand her brother was never coming back. She could not quite comprehend it herself.

An old man, half-shaven and in a vest, emerged from a hallway and told the ringleader to get his arse inside.

What did I do? demanded the boy.

Inside, said the old man.

The boy continued to plead his innocence.

Inside, said the old man in a lower voice.

The quieter he spoke the more threatening he became.

The boy stood his ground and insisted on being informed of the nature of his wrong doing. But the old man had no more patience with the troublesome child. He pulled up his sagging trousers in preparation to carry the brat back into the house.

His cause was hopeless, so the boy relented and did as he was told.

Sorry Mary, said the man.

Dat's alright Mister Goode, said Mary.

Where are ye off ta? he enquired politely, anywhere nice?

Just a little break, said Mary, ta see some relatives in Dublin.

Some time away 'll do ye good, he said.

Yes, repeated Mary, some time away would be good.

There was a sting of guilt in her chest. She was deceiving the old man who was well intentioned and meant no malice. Still she felt compelled to do so. She feared destiny would conspire against her and confound her plans. Or that some force human or unearthly would deter her and she must guard against it.

She walked down the Main Street passed all the tiredly familiar shops and houses. For days the street had been deserted and the shops had been shuttered up. An eerie hush had settled over the place. She was glad of it. After days of frantic activity the tranquillity had the soothing effect of a strong drink. Now the street was becoming busy once more. The grieving was over. She saw the familiar faces loitering and hanging about. Shock and grief had been replaced by an acceptance that the dead were dead and that life went on, must go on regardless. Not through courage, simply because there was no other choice. Mary didn't ponder the matter too deeply. It was not her way. She was too practical and, she finally admitted to herself, too selfish.

She came to the bridge. Across the river was the dormant factory. It had the look of a fallen empire. Apart from a few men guarding the gate it was a city deserted. The chimney stacks had ceased to expel their smoky breath. The quay was bereft of ships and the quayside was abandoned and empty. After the constant and intense hubbub the sight was striking, and Mary had a troubling feeling of loss for the very thing that had killed her brother. So this was the tragic end her mother had so often predicted. First the death of twenty-seven men then the death of the factory. Not one disaster, the town had two disasters to grieve over.

A raw wind was sweeping down the valley. Mary tightened her scarf and hurried on, if she didn't she would be late for her appointment. She came to the fork in the road and forced herself up the incline past the hospital. The sight of the white shingle building brought back the most horrendous memories.

A crowd of broken-hearted relatives had converged upon the gates that terrible morning. Sentries had been stationed and it was impossible for anyone to get through the barrier. People tussled for the attention of the few officials at the gates. No concrete information was available, only a rumour that a handful of workers had been taken alive from the scene of the explosion. It was enough to give hope to many. At long intervals family members were allowed through. They wanted to see their loved ones, even if they were dead. Mary thought it would have been better for most if they had not. The distress they displayed when going in was doubled when they came out. Mary saw the woman called Rose surrounded by comforters, her mouth open as she let out an inaudible scream of anguish. She had two men to cry over, a father and a lover. As for Mary, she had no hope. She waited only to identify her brother.

In the early afternoon, after standing for hours, she spoke to an employee from the factory.

He called out her brother's name.

Yes, said Mary, my brother Michael worked in dat part of de factory.

When was the last time you saw your brother? the man asked.

Mary repeated the question. The last time I saw my brother...*alive*?

The man's pen was hovering over a clipboard. He leaned forward to prompt her.

Yesterday, said Mary, just before his shift started.

The official glanced at the board, made a sharp tick and glanced back at Mary. He was concerned by her remoteness.

Are you alright? he enquired.

I'm fine, said Mary in the same chilly monotone.

This was obviously not the case. She appeared to be in a haze. She was probably in shock. He had been warned by the nurses, some of the bereaved will be unable to stop crying, some won't cry at all.

The young man instructed one of the soldiers to allow her through the barrier.

Is no one with you? he asked, did you come here on your own?

No, no one is with me, said Mary, and she wondered if being alone was in some way strange.

In truth she couldn't remember if she had come alone or was accompanied by someone. She remembered very little of what had occurred over the past twelve hours. She was in a fog. Everything was going on at a distance.

Come this way, said the man.

Mary wondered why he was talking to her like she was a child.

Are you certain you wouldn't prefer to wait for a relative or friend? suggested the man.

Why? asked Mary.

The man stopped at the entrance and turned solemnly to face her.

It was a very powerful explosion, he explained, most of the men were dismembered.

Mary was becoming dizzy and nauseous. She put her hand over her mouth.

Take a seat, said the man, and he guided her to a low wooden bench in the corridor.

Mary sat.

I'll go and get ye a drink, said the man.

Loud moans and wails were coming from somewhere further inside the hospital.

A proper drink, thought Mary, dat's what she needed. Dat would make it all much easier.

Here, have some of this, he said.

The man was beside her and was offering her a cup.

She had a sip. It was water. He took the cup from her hand. He was eager to get the ordeal over with as soon as possible. Delaying would only make it harder for both of them, especially her.

He took her arm and accompanied her down the corridor. Mary looked aimlessly into the wards. Most of the patients were sitting upright in their beds. None of them spoke. A melancholy hung over them. She thought she saw Seanee in a chair by a window. Coming towards her was a tearful family, their heads heavy. Now it was Mary's turn. The young man had disappeared and a doctor was talking to her. His words had to travel a long way to reach her. His lips moved. The sound came eventually and her brain had to decipher its meaning like it was a foreign language she barely understood. After a few sentences she gave up altogether and the doctor also gave up. Then they came to the place where the bodies were. She was trembling and was unable to advance. Why did she have to do this? She must have actually uttered the words because the doctor was answering.

Just to be absolutely certain, he said, and there was a pressure on her lower back to encourage her forward.

The room was brilliant white and dreamlike. Mary doubted it was real. But the hospital smell seeped into her nostrils. This couldn't be imagined. So it was real. A waking nightmare in glowing white. Heaven and hell rolled into one. Trolleys lined the ward. What lay beneath the freshly laundered sheets were not the bodies of men. They were the bits of men. Just body parts in inhuman shapes. Grotesque shattered remnants, burnt up bits and pieces, a jumble, a jigsaw of fragments. Mary heard the nursery rhyme going around in her head.

> *All the king's horses and all the king's men*
> *Couldn't put Michael together again*

The doctor raised the sheet on the first trolley and coaxed her to come nearer.

Is this yer brother? he asked, is dere a distinguishin mark ye recognise?

Mary kept her eyes from the awful thing the doctor had revealed.

She moved like a sleepwalker down the ward, not fully conscious of what was governing her. Near the end she stopped and her shaking hand pointed.

Dat's my brother, she said, dat's my brother Michael.

The doctor was exhausted. He had been through the same agony with half a dozen families already. In many cases determining who was who was an impossible task, but he reminded himself that it had to be done for the sake of the relatives, so he indulged her. They would move onto the next and the next until, he hoped, something was recognised.

He went to the trolley she'd chosen and pinched the sheet and drew it down. The linen stuck to the melted flesh. He peeled it off, exposing the full horror underneath.

Dat's him, said Mary.

Are you absolutely certain? asked the doctor.

Mary shivered and nodded.

How could ye tell it was this trolley? asked the doctor as he replaced the sheet.

He was talking to himself. Mary was moving towards the corridor.

The other man was waiting for her outside. He said there were details regarding the burial to be discussed.

Mary was incapable of replying. In her mind she was still in the ward and the doctor was saying that her brother wouldn't have suffered. But her brother's face told of the most terrible pain.

We can deal with it later on, the man suggested.

Yes, said Mary, later on, we can deal with it later on. The hospital was sweltering. She needed fresh air.

The man followed her dutifully. He was worn out like the doctor and in a few minutes he would have to go through the same trial with the next family.

He said good bye to Mary at the gate, consulted his clipboard and called out the next name.

As Mary passed out through the barrier the crowd was moved to one side. A box wagon was entering the hospital. Its grim load consisted of empty coffins stacked one on top of the other. They were all the same size. All the dead, including Michael, would be accorded a free coffin, a coffin they could only partially fill.

Mary raised the newly polished lion's head and knocked on the front door. The deep gloss was like a black crystal pool and Mary imagined slipping through it into a fairytale world beyond. A figure was lurking behind the net curtain of the bay window. It was watching Mary. The light from the western end of the room produced the vague outline of a woman. Mary thought it was the doctor's wife. She fixed upon her and the figure drew back abruptly.

After a long delay a flustered young maid came running to admit her.

Oh, said the maid, with a stunted gasp.

She was shy and was unsure what words to use.

Won't ye come in, she said, I'm very sorry about yer brother.

Mary removed her scarf, shook her matted hair loose and said thank you.

It's very sad, said the maid, and she darted off into a room down the hall to announce her arrival.

We'll be with her shortly, said the doctor's mother.

The maid had no need to repeat it, the old woman could be heard in the hall and Mary was left to wait in silence in an uncomfortable chair. She had to fight her restlessness. Her mind kept drifting back to that night. It kept intruding upon her, demanding her attention. She felt the rumbling and trembling of the earth again. The first explosion had thrown her out of her bed, then came a second and a third that brought the windows below in. She dressed in a frenzy and tore down the stairs, her boots half-laced. Her father was by the fire. He'd slept in his clothes again. His face wore the horrified expression of fear and dread, of something too awful to contemplate. The front door had been thrown open by the force of the blast. Mary ran out into the street. Mrs Dempsey was in the road in her nightdress and a pair of men's boots, her children gathered about her screaming and crying. Every household was stirring. Mary joined the mad flight of people down towards the bridge. Broken glass was strewn along the Main Street. All the shop windows without shutters were smashed. Everywhere Mary saw panic and despair and confusion. An old man fell on the incline up to the bridge. She left him there and raced on with all the others. Over the bridge they flew, in the sudden cold and wind, mothers, brothers, sisters, friends, fellow workers, fathers, without hats, without coats, one without shoes, a pitiful ramshackle human stampede desperate to get to the scene and terrified at what they would find there. The sky over the north beach was glowing red and yellow. Some ran to the factory gates on the quay. Mary kept onwards, heading for the entrance on the north beach. Many fell off at the second incline after the hospital, the effort to continue without a brief respite was too much. Mary kept running and running. She struggled for breath. Her lungs and throat and nostrils were burning. She tripped on her lace and crashed to the ground. Lumps of skin were torn from her face and her nose was

171

bleeding. She got up, tied her laces carelessly around her ankles and continued on. She turned off the road, went through the pillars and down the tree-lined avenue. The avenue was dark. She was charging into the blackness. She could hear people in front and behind panting and fighting for air. Then came the lights of the entrance. Guards and soldiers were struggling to prevent the mob from entering. Mary took the sandy road along the perimeter of the fence. It was a good half mile distance to the nitro houses. Mary refused to let up. Her heart was near bursting. She cleaned the blood away on her shirt sleeve. The sole of her boot was coming away and she ripped it off. Eventually she reached the breach in the fence. She worked herself through, scratching her back and legs on the broken rusty wires. She scrambled up a bank on her hands and knees, grabbing clumps of long thin reeds. The dune offered no help. It resisted being scaled. The reeds came out at the roots or slipped through her hands slicing her fingers. She fell backwards, tumbled down and began the scramble again. The air all around was hot. Smoke drifted over the top of the dune. There was a hellish light above. Bits of charred and smouldering wood lay everywhere and there was smell like beef in a frying pan.

The nightmare suddenly stopped.

Miss...Miss.

Another maid, with a faint moustache, was looming over her. She was balancing a silver tray of tea in one hand and was poking Mary's shoulder with the other.

Are ye alrye?

What? said Mary.

You were makin' queer noises, said the maid.

Mary blinked.

I was daydreamin, she explained.

Ye surely were, said the maid, and she went into the opposite room.

Mary glimpsed the doctor's wife through the open door. She thought she was sitting on the floor. She looked closer. The woman was perched on a footstool.

The maid plonked the tray noisily on a table and asked if anything else was required.

Catherine looked absently at Mary.

Ask her to come in, she said.

The maid made a grand sweep into the room with her arm and Mary entered.

The maid mumbled something rude about Catherine as she retreated down the hall to her world in the basement directly below.

A sketchbook and pencil were resting on Catherine's lap and the floor was littered with rough drawings. There was a strong scent from fresh lilies on the mantelpiece, but the fire was unlit and Mary felt a chill.

It appears I have overstepped my authority, said Catherine.

Her pencil scratched and slashed across the surface of the paper as she spoke. She was studying Mary and drawing her impression of her.

Apparently so, said Mary.

Will ye be takin your old job back? she asked.

Mary was left searching for the courage to say *no*. Such a small word and yet it was nearly impossible to utter.

She was spared the anxiety.

De answer is no den.

No, echoed Mary softly, just so it had been said, I won't be takin me old position.

The pencil halted mid-stroke and then continued down the page.

Dat's de wisest choice, said Catherine.

I believe so.

Did ye write to my husband by any chance?

173

No, said Mary, he gave me an address to write, I never wrote to him though.

Nothing ta tell anyway, said Catherine, Oscar and I were just friends.

She was lying. Mary had seen the evidence Catherine had tried to hide. But Mary was not inclined to argue, what good would it do?

Oscar has gone, she said.

Yes, said Mary, most of de people have lost dere jobs.

Catherine peered into the far distance. Gangs of men were digging in the debris of the four flattened buildings near the end of the beach.

I wonder if it will ever open again?

Mary approached the window to see better.

Not for tree months at least, she said, dat's what I heard anyway.

I'm sorry ta hear about yer brother.

Mary merely nodded.

I was lyin awake with de curtains open when the explosion happened, said Catherine, and I saw a great fire ball and I raced down to de factory gates. I met a man. He had no arm.

His name was Gallagher, said Mary.

I don't know if he survived.

He died, said Mary.

The pencil was digging into the paper, tearing through it.

I hate this place so much, said Catherine, I hate this pointless, stupid life so much.

It'll be better when yer husband gets back, said Mary.

He's goin ta take me ta London.

It was another lie, or a delusion. Perhaps she did believe it. The old woman wasn't going to let her son go without a fight and the doctor's wife could never win.

We'll rent a house at first I suppose, said Catherine.

174

Mary stepped on one of the discarded drawings on the floor. It was a face distorted in agony. It reminded Mary of her brother's face.

Ye'll tink I'm quite mad when I say dis.

Mary wanted to say she already thought she was quite mad.

It would have made a magnificent paintin.

What would have made a magnificent paintin? asked Mary.

De explosion, said the doctor's wife.

Ye should put a shawl on Mrs O'Connell, said Mary, ye'll catch cauld.

What?

The pencil was working frantically now and she didn't seem to hear Mary as she said goodbye.

The church rang out its dismal chimes. The train would be coming soon. Mary turned off the Main Street towards the station. Just after the church, on the other side of the street, was her mother's shop. The business that once was had lapsed gradually from her conscious mind until it was just another memory diluted in the pool of other even more unhappy memories.

Mary crossed the road. A new pane of glass had been fitted. The workman's greasy paw marks were still to been seen all over it. In the middle of the floor was a neat pile of dirt and rubbish. Her father was out in the yard at the rear. He was leaning on his brush and was talking to himself. He hadn't had a drink since the night of the explosion. It had taken the death of his son to shake him out of it. The abstinence had brought about a change. The devil, and the mean streak that was forever threatening to break out, had departed and he emerged from a long break from reality and was left confused and frightened. Mary put her nose right up to the glass. Some attempt had been made to put the place in order and pretty it up. The walls had been painted a lurid shade of pink. The shelves remained bare, awaiting the new stock. We'll give it a go, her father had said. The possibility that the business might be revived was a happy one. Still Mary thought the odds were against it. The enormous workforce had disappeared. Everywhere you heard predictions of disaster. It would take a miracle to save the town from the inevitable hardship that was coming.

The hefty bag was difficult to carry and it was slowing her down. She cradled it in both her arms and pressed on. A panic began to grip her. If she missed the train she would miss the boat and she was done for. She spurred herself on only to have to stop abruptly. Someone was calling out her name. Mary glanced around and saw no one. It was her mind playing silly tricks on her. Then she heard the chugging of a locomotive. She hitched up the bag and walked faster. She was almost running. But the closer she got to the station the fainter the sound became and when she finally passed through the gates onto the platform, with her arms aching, the noise had completely disappeared.

Mary found herself alone. The serenity gave her a jolt. The workers were always there at that time. Her memory had trained her to expect them. She saw the same spectacle every day from the railway bridge. The narrow strip of platform was like a tiny island heaving with bodies. They crammed every inch from one end to the other. Now the people had vanished and all that remained were echoes calling from the recent past and filled her with a strange yearning. She longed for the pressure of human flesh and not the death and nothingness that seemed to surround her.

She entered the waiting room. The little man behind the mesh screen had his nose stuck in a newspaper and was studying a lengthy article with great interest. Mary deciphered the upside-down headline. It was another report on the explosion. Mary checked the clock above the hatch. The train was almost due. But she couldn't bring herself to interrupt the man, she was too out of sorts, nor could she wait, she was so anxious she thought her insides would burst. She chewed her bottom lip and regarded the little man's immaculate uniform and his clean shaven face. Everything about him proclaimed his efficiency and conscientiousness, everything except his lack of attention to the passenger standing before him.

Eventually her irritation got the better of her and she let her bag fall to the floor. It landed with a thud and the man clutched his chest in fright.

Jaysus, he said, folding the paper quickly and he put it to one side as if it had never been there.

Amien Street Station please, said Mary.

Amien Street, repeated the man.

He was giving his brain a chance to change gears.

Yes, said Mary.

Return? said the man.

Single, said Mary.

The man leaned forward a fraction on his high stool and peered down through the mesh at her tatty luggage.

A single? repeated the man in the hope of drawing out an explanation.

I'm visitin a sick relative, said Mary.

This bit of information was insufficient for the man. A little bit more detail would be required.

I'm not sure when I'm comin back, said Mary, and she offered up the precise fare to indicate that the polite interrogation was over.

The man's curiosity however was still not satisfied and he was preparing to present Mary with another question disguised as friendly conversation.

A single to Amien Street, said Mary impatiently, and she pushed the coins under the screen.

The man squeezed his lips into a tense smile.

Well, ye'll have no difficulties findin a seat, he said forlornly.

No, said Mary taking the ticket, I don't suppose I will, and she stepped away from the hatch.

The precious ticket was spirited away into her coat and she sat down on the hard wooden bench with her bag at her side.

It's runnin fierce late, said the little man, I'd hop on her quare quick when she comes.

Mary nodded and took out an illustrated book she had taken from her brother's room. It remained unopened on her lap while she enjoyed the rhythm of the ticking clock. After a long while she flipped back the cover of the book and flicked aimlessly through the pictures. She was too restless to concentrate on the words. Even as the means of her escape was fast approaching Mary was convinced she would be thwarted. Then a whistle pierced the early autumn air. Mary faltered as she stood. It was just a few short steps to the train but she was overcome with a sudden exhaustion. The weight of the bag was almost more than she could bear. She feared she was going to faint. One foot followed the other out into the strong daylight. She saw the train. It came hissing and puffing up the line. Mary sensed its tremendous mechanical power and it made her own feebleness seem all the more crippling.

She waited until the engine had passed and she went and stood by the platform edge. She looked down the line of empty carriages. A door near the end swung open and before the train had come to a standstill three British soldiers jumped out in quick succession. They tottered onto the platform and laughed drunkenly as they collided with each other. One toppled over completely. Mary recognised the blond haired soldier leering up at her. The other two hauled him to his feet and he bent over and picked up his hat. He dusted it off, tossed it onto his head and slithered up to Mary with the other two in tow.

178

The train was clanking and creaking to a reluctant halt and Mary reached for the handle of the carriage and the safety of a compartment.

Can I 'elp you with that? said the soldier with the blond hair, and he wrestled the bag from her frail grasp.

Be de Jaysus, he said in a ridiculously fake Irish accent, it weighs a feckin ton boy.

The other two soldiers were blocking the door to the compartment.

Mary lunged forward to retrieve the bag and the blond haired soldier shoved her away. In her weakened condition she tumbled over and fell onto her side. Then Mary heard a loud slap followed by a hard bony crack. The blond haired soldier was staggering backwards and was holding the side of his face. An arm was hooked under hers and she was hoisted up and pushed into the carriage. The bag was flung in after her. It was followed by a hard leather case that landed at Mary's feet and the door slammed shut.

FUCKIN WANKER.

FUCKIN BAS-TARD. YE FUCKIN CUNT.

The train was creaking and clanking into motion once more. Oscar was in the opposite seat. He was panting and the right side of his mouth and his cheek was bruised. He pulled a hip flask from his breast pocket. His hand was shaking as he unscrewed the top. It fell and the whiskey was pouring out in little spurts.

Mary whisked it up.

Here, she said.

He put the flask in the left side of his mouth and took one long draught. The golden liquid was dribbling down his chin onto his jacket. He wiped it off and discovered two buttons had been ripped off. He was pulling at a dangling thread where one of his missing buttons used to be.

I just bought de damn ting, he explained, and he asked Mary to open the window.

Mary tugged it down a fraction and the stuffy compartment filled with cool air and the music of the wheels on the track.

Would ye like a cigarette? asked Oscar.

She drew one out from the crushed packet. The cigarette was bent and wrinkled. Mary didn't care, it tasted sweet and warm and comforting.

Are you goin ta London? asked Oscar.

Yes? said Mary, and yerself?

Yes, said Oscar, and he tipped the tiny flask in her direction.

Just a little one ta steady me nerves, she replied, and she took a sip from the silver container.

The alcohol started doing its work immediately and the warm glow she had come to enjoy so much was radiating out from her abdomen and into her limbs. And a tiredness, not of the body but of the heart and soul, overtook her. Her eyelids fell, she drifted off and for a few short minutes she was tranquil. Then the trembling of the earth returned and the nightmare began again. She was struggling up the sand dune. The air was filled with hot dust and smoke and it stuck in her nostrils and her throat. She was on top of the mound. She tumbled down the other side of the dune, her feet sinking deep into the sand. At the bottom of the hill was a body. It was a large man, far bigger than her brother. All the man's clothes had been burnt and he was naked. Beams of light shot about everywhere. Men with torches followed the sound of moans. The mangled remains were found here and there amongst the charred and smouldering bits of wood, melted steel and iron, twisted girders and upturned bogies. Victims rushed by on stretchers. They screamed in agony from their terrible wounds. She looked at the men and said her brother's name but in the darkness and confusion it was impossible to identify one blackened figure from another. She tried to call out his name. The

180

dust in her throat silenced her. Some torches turned towards the shoreline. Painful groans were heard near the water. A small man was found alive. Lights fell upon a horse with its steaming guts hanging out and its skull shattered. Someone was wading into the sea further along. He grabbed a hold of something and was dragging it back to dry land. There was a moment of hope. She saw a limp body, around its neck was a red scarf. And then the final horror as her brother was drawn up onto the beach, a torso with no legs.

She woke with a start. Oscar was looking at her. Slowly, and with some effort, his sad face was transformed into a broad smile and he rubbed her knee in a kindly, affectionate way.

I'll look after you, he said, I've many friends in London.

Tank you, said Mary.

The train was rolling effortlessly away from the town and the dreadful soldiers. Every second put the incident at the station further and further away. Soon it would fade. The other wounds would take much longer to heal.

They came to a bridge. The water below was dark brown and full of earth from the previous night's downpour. It surged through the arches and Mary imagining plunging into the maelstrom. The river would carry her to the open sea and she would be with her mother and brother.

Printed in Great Britain
by Amazon